continued . . .

Killer Swell

A NOAH BRADDOCK NOVEL

JEFF SHELBY

AN ONYX BOOK

ONYX
Published by New American Library, a division of
Penguin Group (USA) Inc., 375 Hudson Street,
New York, New York 10014, USA
Penguin Group (Canada), 90 Eglinton Avenue East, Suite 700, Toronto,
Ontario M4P 2Y3, Canada (a division of Pearson Penguin Canada Inc.)
Penguin Books Ltd., 80 Strand, London WC2R 0RL, England
Penguin Ireland, 25 St. Stephen's Green, Dublin 2,
Ireland (a division of Penguin Books Ltd.)
Penguin Group (Australia), 250 Camberwell Road, Camberwell, Victoria 3124,
Australia (a division of Pearson Australia Group Pty. Ltd.)
Penguin Books India Pvt. Ltd., 11 Community Centre, Panchsheel Park,
New Delhi - 110 017, India
Penguin Group (NZ), cnr Airborne and Rosedale Roads, Albany,
Auckland 1310, New Zealand (a division of Pearson New Zealand Ltd.)
Penguin Books (South Africa) (Pty.) Ltd., 24 Sturdee Avenue,
Rosebank, Johannesburg 2196, South Africa

Penguin Books Ltd., Registered Offices:
80 Strand, London WC2R 0RL, England

Published by Onyx, an imprint of New American Library,
a division of Penguin Group (USA) Inc. Previously published in a Dutton edition.

First Onyx Printing, June 2006
10 9 8 7 6 5 4 3 2 1

For Hannah Elizabeth

 *1*

Marilyn Crier peered in the window, and I knew the past was about to kick me in the ass.

I was sitting at a small table near the front of the SandDune, a cramped and noisy bar in Mission Beach, a block north of the old roller coaster and a block east of the Pacific Ocean. The pub is sandwiched between ten other beach-themed saloons on Mission Boulevard and draws the same crowds. Half yuppie, half nowhere to go. Everyone is tan, the floors are covered with sand and peanut shells, and you can't hear the ocean over the din of music and conversation. But on good nights, you can smell the salt in the air.

Marilyn had called me and said she needed a private investigator. She didn't mention that we hadn't seen each other in over a decade, that she'd despised me when I dated her daughter in high school, or that she'd orchestrated our breakup.

Had to admit I was curious.

We agreed to meet at the SandDune because she said it was on her way home. I couldn't figure out how that might be true, as she didn't work and she lived on the wealthiest side of Mount Soledad over in La Jolla, a world away from the beer and party crowd of the San Diego beach bars. But it was only a couple of blocks from my apartment, and I didn't have to put away my surfboard too early in order to meet her at seven.

I was sipping my beer and following the Padres game on the television monitors when I spotted Marilyn Crier outside the window.

She glanced up above the faux saloon doors, probably checking to make sure she was in the right place. Her green eyes were identical to her daughter's, pale and deep. She looked back in the window, and I waved at her, rising out of my chair. She stared at me for a moment, as if making sure it was me, then nodded and came into the bar. Her red Chanel suit was as out of place as a cat in a giraffe's mouth, but she didn't seem to notice.

She stood at my table, her thin lips in a tight smile. "Noah Braddock," she said, shaking her head slightly. "You haven't changed at all."

I had, but not in ways Marilyn Crier would notice. I did, after all, look pretty much the same, just a little older. I was in a navy T-shirt and white cotton shorts, worn leather sandals on my feet. My hairstyle hadn't changed since high school, still cut short for low maintenance. And I knew she was thinking my tan was too dark for me to be working hard. She had said something similar to me when I was eighteen, but I couldn't recall her exact words.

We shook hands, and I gestured at the empty wooden chair across from me. She continued to look at me as she sat down, silently sizing me up. I did the same. Her blond hair was still blond, no trace of gray despite the fact that she had to be in her mid-fifties by now. It was cut short, blunt, tucked behind her ears. She was still petite, like her daughter, and she reminded me of those plastic-looking news anchors you see on television.

"Mrs. Crier," I said, smiling. "It's good to see you."

She laughed quietly, waving a perfectly manicured hand in my direction. "Noah. I think it's okay if you call me Marilyn now. You're not in high school anymore."

I shrugged. Old habits. You should always be polite to the parents of the girl you desperately want to have sex with in high school.

The girl behind the bar came over, and Marilyn ordered a glass of white wine. The girl didn't laugh, but I figured she might be gone awhile trying to find a bottle.

Marilyn eyed the inhabitants at the bar for a moment and then looked at me, clearing her throat. "Are you living down here?"

I recognized the condescension in her voice, but ignored it. "Couple blocks down, on Jamaica."

"You were a surfer, weren't you?"

"Still am."

She nodded, again taking in my appearance. "I guess you are."

The waitress came back with the glass of wine. I wondered where she found the glass. Marilyn tasted the wine, didn't spit it out, and placed her purse in her lap, settling in. "I'll try not to waste your time, Noah," she said, folding her hands on the table. "Kate is missing."

Hearing Kate's name did something to my stomach. I hadn't seen her since she'd left for college. She'd headed off to Princeton; I'd stayed around to go to San Diego State. In the eleven years since I'd last seen her, I hadn't forgotten Kate Crier.

"Kate's missing," I repeated, turning the beer glass slowly on the table.

Marilyn nodded tersely. "For about a week. She came down for the Fourth. We went to Catalina, did some shopping, things seemed normal."

Kate and I had gone to the Crier family's Catalina Island condo on prom night. And she broke my heart there two months later.

"She was supposed to catch a plane to go home to San Francisco on the eighth," Marilyn continued, the lines at the corners of her mouth tightening. "But she didn't."

A dull roar went up from the bar, and I glanced up at the television. Padres had scored. First time in July.

"She didn't get on the plane?" I asked, looking back to Marilyn.

She shook her head, the pearls in her earlobes jiggling. "No. Randall called when she didn't arrive in San Francisco."

"Randall?"

Marilyn took another micro sip from the glass and fixed her eyes on mine. "Kate's husband."

I raised my eyebrows. "Ah."

"He's a doctor in the Bay area," she said.

She didn't need to add "and you're not." Her tone implied it.

I tried to be mature. "But she didn't get on the plane?"

Marilyn nodded. "I checked with the airline. She never checked in."

The crowd at the bar groaned and I glanced up to see the end of the double play finishing the Padres' half of the inning. That was more like it.

"I got your name from Jack Meyers," Marilyn told me, leaning slightly forward. "He said you assisted him a year ago. He said you're very good."

I'd found Jack Meyers's wife screwing his attorney after three nights of tailing her. When I told him, he thanked me profusely, placed her clothes in a cardboard box, and lit the box on fire. We watched the burning mass float in his backyard pool as he wrote me a check.

I wondered if it hurt for Marilyn Crier to admit that I was good at something. I knew it had to hurt to be sitting in a bar with me.

"So you want me to find her," I said, finishing my beer and setting the mug on the table. "Find Kate."

She stared at me for a moment, perhaps trying to make me squirm like she had when I was in high school. I resisted the urge.

"Noah, I know you don't like me," she said, her eyes even and her voice flat. "But you don't have to like me to help me. I recognized your name when Jack mentioned it. I need an investigator and I figured it might be helpful to have someone do this who knows Kate. Things may not have worked out with Kate way back when . . ."

"And that just crushed you, didn't it, Marilyn?" I said, smiling, but not bothering to warm it up. "I mean, I know you just dreamed of having me for a son-in-law."

She paused for a moment, then folded her hands on the table. "As I was saying, your relationship with Kate didn't work out. But I know you cared about Kate. And I was hoping that might still count for something."

Another groan went up at the bar, but I didn't look up. I stared at Marilyn Crier, but I saw Kate's face. The one that had made high school bearable for me. The face that I used to look to for sympathy as I sat on the bench during high school basketball games. The face attached to the first female body that I saw naked. The face that crushed me that night on Catalina. The face that was going to let my past do a little ass kicking.

So against my better judgment, I told Marilyn Crier that my caring for her daughter did, in fact, still count for something.

 2

I ordered another beer, waited for it to arrive, and then asked Marilyn, "Why would Kate disappear?"

She hesitated and then shook her head. "I don't know."

"Things with Randall are okay?"

She fiddled with one of the gold buttons that ran down the middle of her suit and glanced around the bar. "Randall is wonderful."

"Not what I asked."

Marilyn chuckled and shook her head. "Maybe I made a mistake in coming to you, Noah."

I nodded, thinking the same thing. "I've been wondering if I should put that on my business cards."

She leaned across the table. "Kate loves Randall. You won't be able to turn this into a 'win her back' contest. She loves him."

I took a long swallow from the beer and stared at her without saying anything. I tried to recall the name of the cartoon superhero who could shoot lasers out of his eyes because, at that moment, I really would've liked to use those lasers on Marilyn Crier.

"I am not interested in a 'win her back' contest," I said, finally, setting the glass down and moving closer to the table to meet her gaze. "I'm an investigator, so in order to do the investigating, I normally ask questions." I paused, watching her lean back, away from me. "I asked if things with Randall were okay because it's what you ask when a married person disappears. You investigate—there's that word again—the missing person's relationships first."

I sat back in my chair, exhaling and folding my arms across my chest. I momentarily wished I'd had the guts to speak like that to her in high school.

"I'm sorry," Marilyn said, nodding tersely in my direction. "I was rude."

"Yeah. You were."

"It won't happen again." She paused and then refolded her hands on the table. "Their marriage is . . . a work in progress."

"What the hell does that mean?"

"It means their marriage is no different than anyone else's. They have their good times and their bad times."

I stood up, angry with myself for having entertained the thought that I could work for Marilyn Crier. I had hated her in high school, and the eleven years that had passed hadn't changed my feelings. So much for maturity.

"This isn't gonna happen," I said, fishing some

money out of my pocket. "In order to find a person, Marilyn, I need straight answers. About everything. You'll be better off telling this story, whatever it is, to someone you won't be embarrassed to tell it to."

I tossed several bills on the table and avoided looking at her. I walked away from the table and headed out of the bar. The gas fumes and salty haze were stifling in the evening air as I headed up Mission toward my place.

"Noah! She needs help!"

I slowed to a stop, listening to horns honking as cars cruised the boulevard. Kids leaned out of windows, waving at one another, their faces illuminated by the moon and streetlights. I turned around slowly.

Marilyn walked quickly to me, her face as tight as a drum. But her eyes were different than they'd been. Worry now invaded them.

"She needs help," she repeated, clearly struggling for what to say. "I'm not sure what the problem is. I don't know if she's hiding. I don't know much about her marriage, but I do know there are some things she is unhappy about." She stopped, catching her breath, glancing at the line of cars moving slowly along the street. She looked back to me. "I need your help—to find her and to see if she's okay."

I shoved my hands in the pockets of my shorts, her words making me uncomfortable. If she wanted my help, there was probably a reason to think Kate might be in trouble. Marilyn probably would've been happy never hearing my name again. But here she was.

I looked past her at the roller coaster that dominated the Mission Beach skyline, rising high above the street. Small dots of light illuminated the tracks against the black night. Kate and I had ridden the coaster on our first date.

"Where's Randall?" I asked.

"He's here. He's staying at the La Valencia," she said, her voice relaxing at my interest. "He's been here since Sunday."

I nodded absently, watching the coaster cars crest the top of the tracks and dive to the bottom, the elated screams of the riders echoing down the boulevard.

"I'll start with him," I told her.

"So you'll help me then?" Marilyn asked, gratefulness almost creeping into her voice.

The screams on the coaster died as the hydraulic brakes screeched and cracked in the dark, the ride coming to an end.

"No," I said, moving my gaze to Marilyn's eyes, wanting her to see my face. "But I'll try to help Kate."

 **3**

Marilyn Crier wrote me a check for two thousand dollars on the spot and assured me she would pay whatever it took to find Kate. I assured her I would ask for more money if I needed it. I also explained to her that I would be around asking questions and if she got uncooperative, my services would come to a halt without refund. She said she understood, told me Randall's last name was Tower, and walked to her silver BMW 530i, edging it carefully out into the traffic and disappearing into the sea of cars.

I wondered why she hadn't contacted the police first and probably should have asked that question. But Marilyn hadn't mentioned any danger, just that Kate was having some problems. I felt certain that she came to me first because involving the authorities would've meant drawing the kind of attention that families like the Criers did everything in their power to avoid.

I crossed Mission Boulevard, cut down an alley, and

headed north on the boardwalk. The moon was shining on the small, gentle waves, and the sand looked bright white because of it. Couples strolled along the walk; kids hung out on the beach, smoking and feeling adult, their small bonfires dotting the shoreline.

I remembered hanging out at the beach in high school. It was a safe haven for teenagers. You could smoke a cigarette, drink a can of beer, or make out with a girl and feel like no one was watching, the ocean serving as a giant security blanket of noise and privacy.

I ducked my head under the breeze, my chin digging into my chest. Kate and I had spent a lot of nights at the beach. She always told her parents we were at the movies or shopping. They didn't like the thought of us going to those places either, but they seemed less illicit than the sand and water. Of course, my alcoholic mother, the father I had never known, the tiny house in Bay Park, and my penchant for spending more time on a surfboard than in class provided plenty for them to disapprove of.

I hopped the wall into the small courtyard at the back of my house and slid open the glass door to the living room, shutting it behind me. My place is small, a one-bedroom bungalow built in the 1930s with wood floors and the permanent smell of wax. Four of us had lived here during college, two bunk beds in the one bedroom. Everyone had left but me. The old couple that owned it dropped the rent for me when I graduated and left me alone. It was a steal for the price, and you can't beat eating your breakfast as you head down the sand to the early morning waves, which I tried to do most every day.

I grabbed a Red Trolley Ale from the fridge and collapsed on the sofa. A knot had formed in my stomach, and I didn't like it. It surprised me that Marilyn hadn't asked me how I had become an investigator, but I figured that would've been too much interest in me for her. She would've loved to hear how it took me six years to finish college, that I waited tables for two years after that until I'd spotted an ad in the paper for an insurance company looking to train an investigator. I liked the job, the freedom of the hours, the solitary environment. I didn't like the reports, the suits I had to wear to the office, or the fact that I had a supervisor. I completed my hours, applied for my license from the state, and said adios. Not glamorous, not lucrative, but it had become my life and I had grown to appreciate it.

Marilyn probably would not, and that made me smile in the darkness of my living room as I sipped the beer.

 **4**

I left the beer half empty on my coffee table, dug around in the piles of laundry for my car keys, and headed out to pay Randall Tower a visit.

I found my Jeep in the alley, turned down Jamaica, forced my way onto Mission, and settled in for the snaillike cruise up to La Jolla. The police had tried to crack down on the cruising by employing curfews, roadblocks, whatever they could think of. Nothing worked with any degree of success so the cops had become content with just patrolling, making sure all were behaving themselves.

I passed the Catamaran Hotel, moving into Pacific Beach. PB had recently moved itself into the upper class of San Diego beach communities, adding trendy restaurants and nightclubs to the beachfront hotels that sat between Grand and Garnett. The clothing switched from long shorts and T-shirts to polo shirts and sundresses, and the cars on the street increased in price.

The traffic lightened as I swung around the curve onto La Jolla Boulevard and into the area known as Bird Rock. The houses hung off the cliffs protected by elaborate gates and hedges. An elite area of rich people who didn't like you to see them while they watched the ocean from their living rooms.

I moved through Bird Rock and parked at the very southern end of Prospect Street, near the Museum of Contemporary Art. If you lived in La Jolla, Prospect Street was downtown. Forget that the rest of San Diego referred to the harbor area about fifteen miles to the south with its high-rises and international airport as downtown. If I'd needed directions to the La Valencia hotel, Marilyn Crier would've said, "It's right in the middle of downtown."

A pink place of lodging sounds obnoxious, but the La Valencia was able to pull it off. The luxury resort took up half a block on Prospect, sitting atop the cove with sweeping northern views of La Jolla Shores and Torrey Pines. Charge three hundred bucks a night for a room and you can put polka dots on the outside and it will still be chic.

Two young high school students in tuxedo shirts, bow ties, and black shorts hustled around the valet stand, parking expensive foreign cars. I walked through the courtyard, wondering how much the meals cost that were being served on the outdoor patio. More than they were worth, I figured.

The front desk was a small, oak-encased area off the main hall. The door at the end of the hall was open, the

Pacific sparkling out in the distance. Expensive perfume and cologne mingled in the air above the antique furniture in the lobby. I probably should've worn a jacket, but that would've looked silly over my T-shirt and shorts.

The gentleman behind the desk wore a dark suit and tie over a light blue dress shirt. His blond hair was slicked back off his forehead, and he didn't cringe when I stepped to the desk.

"I'm here for Randall Tower," I said, smiling.

The clerk managed to look me up and down before I realized he'd done it. "He's a guest, sir?"

"That's what I was told."

He nodded, as if he already knew he was correct. "I can't give out room information, sir."

I nodded, as if I already knew that. "Can you ring his room?"

He thought about it, which I understood because it was a tough question. "Your name, sir?"

"Braddock."

"Is he expecting you?"

"I have no idea. Possibly."

His eyebrows arched, and I hoped he hadn't pushed the secret alarm button beneath the desk.

"Sir, our guests expect a certain amount of privacy," he began, sounding as if he were reading from a brochure. "If you'd like to leave a message—"

"I wouldn't," I said, cutting him off and smiling. "Please let him know a friend of his wife's is here."

Now the eyebrows knitted, concern frosting his eyes. He was clearly casting me for the jilted lover or other man, or some other figure in the dramas that play out in rich people's lives.

"Sir, I really . . ." he began, puffing his chest out.

"Let's not make this silly," I said. "I'm here to help the guy, not cause trouble. So either you can ring his room and tell him Noah Braddock is here and wants to see him, or I can start going floor to floor, room to room until I find him."

He bristled and lifted his chin. "Or I can throw you out of the hotel."

I smiled. "You personally?"

His cheeks reddened slightly. "I meant, I would call the police and have you removed from the premises."

"Right," I said. I reached into my pocket, pulled out my wallet, flipped it open to my license, and laid it on the counter. "Call the police. They're friends of mine. I can give you a couple of names to ask for specifically. I'm sure they'd be happy to respond to a case where you simply wouldn't dial a room number. I'm sure they'd see your side of it."

The color in his cheeks brightened, and he pursed his lips, glancing at my license but not wanting to stare at it. He looked back at me, knowing he was beaten.

"Tower, you said?" he said, straightening his tie and trying to regain his dignity.

I grabbed my wallet and deposited it back in my pocket. "You got it."

He picked up the receiver, punched several numbers on the console in front of him, and shook his head. "I hate this place."

I smiled, feeling sorry for him. "You and me both, pal. You and me both."

 5

I was standing at the open back door of the lobby, admiring the sparkling black evening ocean when a finger tapped me on the shoulder.

"Mr. Braddock?" he asked as I turned around. "I'm Randall Tower."

Randall was slightly taller than me, maybe six-four, and movie-star handsome. His thick, dark hair was cut stylishly short on the sides, a longer shock combed off his bronze forehead. Bright blue eyes rested above a very Waspy nose, thick lips, and a dimpled chin. A black cotton dress shirt and white linen slacks hung loosely on his thin frame. Black loafers covered his feet.

He offered his hand, and his grip was stronger than I expected.

"Noah," I said.

He nodded, a small smile turning up a corner of his mouth. "Marilyn said I might be hearing from you."

"That's funny?"

He waved a hand in the air. "Marilyn said to watch out for ulterior motives. Those were her exact words, I believe."

"I'm sure they were."

He aimed a thumb back over his shoulder. "Buy you a drink?"

I nodded and followed him through the lobby into a small room that housed a bar and half a dozen stools, all empty. Apparently, in expensive hotels you didn't hang out in the bar. Maybe you had the bartender hang out in your room.

We sat at the farthest end of the bar. I ordered a Jack and Coke, and Randall asked for a Heineken. The small man behind the bar had the drinks on the bar in less than thirty seconds and then moved away from us. Probably didn't want my T-shirt to rub off on him.

"You knew Kate?" Randall asked me.

"In high school."

"Marilyn said you dated."

"We did."

He chuckled, his eyes amused. "So are there ulterior motives that I should be aware of?"

"Nope. Marilyn hired me to find Kate. That's my motive."

He eyed me for a moment. "Sure about that?"

I stared back. "Yeah. I promise that if I find Kate, I won't ask her to go to the prom with me," I said. "Believe it or not, I have moved on since high school."

He nodded. "Good."

Something in the way he said it made me think that

he was telling me that if I did have other reasons for taking on the case, I could forget them. Kate was his. It shouldn't have, but it irritated me.

"How long have you been married?" I asked, sipping the drink.

"Three years," he told me, his eyes focused on the green beer bottle. "We met at Stanford. Kate was finishing her master's and I'd just completed my internship at the hospital."

"You're a doctor."

"Orthopedic surgeon," he said. "I'm practicing now at St. Andrew's in San Francisco."

"That's where you live?"

He took a drink from the bottle and nodded. "Yeah. North of the city in Marin County."

Randall and Kate were making some big bucks to live in one of the most expensive counties in the country.

We didn't speak for nearly a minute, the silence in the bar broken by the bartender's polishing of the brass rail that ran the length of the bar. A quiet shushing sound.

"Enough of the small talk," he said, suddenly, his voice serious. "I hate small talk. It's what I do with Marilyn."

I raised my glass in his direction. "You said it, not me."

"You're an investigator?"

"I am."

"Can you find Kate?"

"I don't really know enough about what's going on to give you a good answer to that," I told him.

He thought about that and stared at his Heineken. His eyes were elsewhere, though. "I don't think she wants to be married anymore," he said.

"Why's that?"

He laughed, shaking his head. "Because that's basically what she told me."

I didn't react right away because I felt bad for him. No matter the state of their marriage, hearing that had to hurt. I remembered her conversation with me on Catalina and feeling as if someone had just died.

"Someone else?" I finally said.

He hesitated for a moment, glancing at me as if I'd asked an unexpected question. Then he looked back at the beer bottle. "I don't think so. I think she just doesn't want to be married."

I found that odd. "So why would that make her disappear?"

He held the neck of the beer bottle loosely between his fingers, swinging it back and forth. "Not sure. We've been arguing, though."

"About?"

"Oh, everything, I guess," he said, a frustrated expression on his face. "We can't get along. I get mad at her, she gets mad at me. Neither of us can please the other."

I nodded. "When was the last time you spoke to her?"

"The night before her flight was supposed to leave. She seemed fine, said she was looking forward to getting home after being down here for a few days," Randall said. "That was it. When she didn't show up and no one had heard from her, I flew down right away."

I finished my drink, and we walked back to the lobby. We shook hands again.

"Thanks for doing this," he said, giving a quick nod.

"No problem," I replied. "You're staying in San Diego for a while?"

"As long as I need to," he said, a weak smile creasing his face.

I said I'd be in touch and walked outside. The valets were talking and laughing. They glanced at me and then went back to their conversation. Guess I didn't look like I owned a car they would consider parking.

Dr. Randall Tower hadn't given me much. Normal marriage problems, seemed surprised that Kate would take off. But one thing bothered me as I walked back along Prospect to my car.

He seemed pretty calm for a guy who hadn't seen his wife in nearly two weeks.

6

Marilyn had told me that Kate had stayed at the San Diego Marriott Hotel and Marina during her visit to the city. Marilyn explained that Kate always stayed at a hotel when she came home, saying she didn't want to be a bother to her parents, despite their objections. I wondered how Marilyn explained that one to her socialite friends as I made the drive to the hotel to see if there were any giant clues to trip over.

The Marriott sits at the southern edge of the downtown area, sandwiched between the revitalized Gaslamp Quarter and the finger of San Diego Bay that separates the mainland from Coronado Island. The two towers of the hotel jut into the horizon like glass spears, and the lights from the Coronado Bridge reflected off the mirrored exteriors in the bluish-black evening sky.

The girl at the front desk of the Marriott was less wary than the guy at the La Valencia, and, after a quick look at my license, she gave me what little info on Kate she had.

"The reservation was from the second through the eighth, but she checked out two days early," she said, staring at the computer screen. "Bill paid in full."

"Room been rented since?"

She nodded quickly. "Several times. We're running close to full." She frowned, obviously not appreciating San Diego's push toward tourism. "It's like that in the summer."

"Anything else on the bill?"

She studied the screen, then shook her head. "Nope. Room and tax. That's it."

I thanked her for her help and wandered around the lobby. I glanced in the windows of the gift shops that lined the walkway to the outdoor courtyard. I saw expensive things. I poked my head into the bar and observed the noise and commotion. Nothing pointed me in the right direction.

I walked outside to my car and was heading toward the exit on Harbor when a solitary car at the end of the lot caught my eye. The red Mercedes was parked diagonally, taking up two spaces, shining brightly beneath a towering streetlamp. There were small dents on top of the trunk, as if someone had pounded a fist into it.

I made a U-turn and parked next to the car. I stared at the car for a moment before getting out.

I have always been baffled by my actions. I don't know why I stuck a straw up the cat's nose when I was six. I don't know why I took my first drink at fifteen. I

don't know why I sometimes stop talking to friends
for no reason. For as long as I can remember, I have
done things simply because I felt compelled. No justi-
fication, no reason. I just do things.

That Mercedes was screaming for me to look at it.

I stepped out of my car and the smell hit me almost
immediately. I swallowed hard against whatever was
rotting in the area and walked up to the driver's side
window. A white leather purse was tossed casually
into the backseat. The keys were in the ignition.

I tried the doors, but they were locked. The stench
was smothering me, and I couldn't ignore the fact that
it was coming from the trunk. I pulled the tire iron
from the rear of my Jeep and wedged it into the space
between the trunk door and the body of the car. I jim-
mied the iron up and down for a minute before I heard
the lock snap. I pushed up on it. The lid creaked
slightly as it rose.

The odor emerged like a nuclear cloud, and I took a
step back, the muscles in my throat convulsing. I held
my forearm in front of my nose and mouth and looked
reluctantly into the trunk.

Kate Crier's face stared back at me, the life in it long
gone.

 7

The cops were unrolling yellow crime-scene tape like birthday streamers when Detective Liz Santangelo arrived just before eleven. She wore a white blouse under a black leather jacket, black jeans shimmying up her long legs, and open-heel sandals on her feet. The jacket was gathered at her waist, accentuating her figure, and more than a few of the twenty or so cops now on the scene tried to eye her inconspicuously as she strode in my direction.

Since I'd seen her naked a couple of years ago, the thrill was gone for me.

She strode right up to me and spread her hands out in front of her, palms up, and said, "You opened the trunk. Why?"

In my head, I kept replaying the moment I'd opened the trunk. I couldn't make it stop. "I didn't know she was in there, Liz."

She narrowed her blue eyes beneath her jet-black

hair. "You thought the smell was what, an old sand-wich?"

Liz's beauty was matched only by her sarcasm. "Gimme a break, Liz."

She shook her head and folded her arms across her chest, disappointing much of the crowd. Her hair was pulled back away from her face, a small silver hoop in each earlobe. Her thin, pink lips were somewhere be-tween a frown and a snarl. And her eyes could be hypnotizing, particularly when they were rolling.

"Noah, you know better," she said, shaking her head. "This is junior varsity stuff." She stared at me for a moment and her expression changed. "You know her?"

I nodded. "Kate Crier."

Liz's eyes blinked, she stood up a little straighter, and she glanced at the car. "Kate?"

I nodded and Liz frowned, her chin dropping slightly. Liz had been two years ahead of Kate and me in school. It occurred to me that they might've played volleyball together, but I wasn't sure.

"Shit," Liz said quietly. "Why are you here?"

I let out a deep breath. "Her mother hired me to find her."

"They thought she was missing?"

"Yeah, I don't think anyone knew she was in the trunk," I said sharply, irritated by everything.

She stared at me with a hard look I'd become all too familiar with during our six-month relationship two years ago. The look was a mixture of condescension, disgust, and confusion. I always bring out the best in women.

"Be right back," she said.

She walked over to the cops stringing the tape, pointing at several spots that she wanted secured. She then made her way over to the medical examiner's people. Beneath the bright police lights that bit into the darkness, they were taking Kate's body from the car. I turned away. I knew that I would never be able to remember Kate as the gorgeous eighteen-year-old high school senior again. She would always be looking at me from the inside of that trunk.

"Noah," Liz said, back at my side. "What else do you know?"

I shook my head. "Not much. I talked to her mother and her husband earlier tonight."

She nodded and watched over my shoulder at what I assumed to be the removal of the corpse. I closed my eyes and tried to flush the image of Kate's dead face from my memory.

"I'm gonna need you to make a statement," Liz said, as I opened my eyes.

"Tomorrow," I said, exhausted. "I'll come down in the morning."

"Tonight," she said, the hard cop look returning to her face. "You'll make the statement tonight. I don't want to miss anything."

I had never appreciated the fact that Liz could turn

her cop behavior off and on so easily. More often than not, it was the cop behavior that I had to deal with in our relationship, and that had never worked for me.

I stared at her for a moment, and she held my gaze. Then I said, "Now I remember."

The corners of her mouth twitched. "Remember?"

"Why we broke up. I remember why now."

Her eyes went flat, and she glanced over my shoulder again. "Really. Why's that?"

"Because I decided you were a bitch," I said, and walked away.

 8

I gave my statement and left without speaking to Liz again. I knew I'd been out of line but I wasn't quite ready to apologize yet. I figured there would be another opportunity in the too near future.

I drove away from downtown and headed north toward La Jolla, to Marilyn Crier's house. I had found Kate, and I figured I should let her know, if the police hadn't already beaten me to it. I wasn't looking forward to the conversation, but I owed her that much.

Mount Soledad has two sides. The south side is considered Pacific Beach, the homes looking back at Mission Bay. Once you passed the giant cross that emerged from the top of the hill, you were in La Jolla. The mansions jutted out from the side of the mountain with views that spanned the coastline. You could almost smell the money.

The Criers' home rested just below the cross, a gated enclave that laughed at everything below it. The gate was open as I approached the drive, a police car turning out of the property and passing me in the opposite direction.

Marilyn was standing in front of the giant oak doors of her house between two huge white pillars, illuminated by the coach lights. Her arms were crossed tightly across her chest, and her chin was tucked down. Ken Crier, her husband and Kate's father, stood next to her, his face as white as a sheet.

I stopped my car in the circular drive and got out.

Marilyn looked up as I approached. "Noah." Her voice was hoarse and disjointed.

I held up my hand, an awkward attempt at a greeting. "The police were just here?"

She nodded slightly. "Yes."

"I'm sorry, Marilyn."

Marilyn's lips puckered, and her eyes filled with tears. She turned and disappeared through the massive doors into the house.

Ken Crier walked down the stone steps. He cleared his throat and extended his hand. "Noah. It's been a long time."

Ken was a small, compact man with thinning brown hair. His eyes were small, his mouth perpetually tightened into what looked like an uncomfortable grimace. Large forearms extended from the sleeves of his white golf shirt, which was tucked tightly into a pair of immaculate khakis. In eleven years, he'd aged about an hour.

I shook his hand. "Yeah. I wish I were here for a different reason."

He cleared his throat again, his eyes unsteady. "You spoke with Marilyn earlier?"

"Yes."

He nodded and pinched the bridge of his nose. "Did the police tell you anything?"

"No. Not really."

He sighed and shook his head. "It's unbelieveable. I don't know that I believe it."

He was in shock, and I didn't know what to say to him. I had never been able to speak comfortably with him. He'd intimidated the hell out of me as a teenager, always cutting me off in mid-sentence and making me feel small. It was his way. But I'd always known that he loved his daughter. I hadn't seen Kate in years and her death was digging into me like an ice pick; I couldn't imagine what Ken was feeling.

"Noah, I'd like your help," he said, suddenly.

"My help?"

He nodded at me, his eyes beginning to refocus. "I need to know what happened to Kate."

I squinted into the evening breeze. "I'm sure the police will keep you informed."

He waved a hand in the air, dismissively. The wrinkles around his eyes tightened in contempt. "The police will take their time, tell me things I don't understand, and treat me like an idiot." He paused. "I don't need that and I don't want that."

"I don't know that I can do much better," I told him honestly.

"I'd appreciate it if you'd try," he replied, turning toward the house. He walked back up the stairs and stopped at the giant doors. He turned back to me. "She was in trouble, Noah."

That surprised me because it was at odds with what Marilyn had told me. "Trouble?"

He bit his bottom lip for a moment, and his eyes blinked quickly. "Something was wrong," he said, his voice tight. "This wasn't random. I knew something was wrong with her or with her life. I could feel it. But she wouldn't talk to me."

Kate could be stubborn, but I remembered her being Daddy's little girl. "Why?"

He turned toward the open doors, then paused. "She never forgave me," he said, over his shoulder.

"For what?"

Ken Crier turned back and looked at me. There was little warmth in his smile. "For always intruding in her life."

 *9*

"I lied," Kate Crier had said to me.

It was a July night, two months after our high school graduation. We were sitting on a bench on the board-walk on Catalina Island. We'd had dinner at a small Italian place, near the casino at the north end of the is-land.

I didn't know what she was talking about.

"What?" I said. "You lied?"

She took a deep breath and brushed the blond bangs from her tan forehead.

"You asked me earlier if I was alright," she said. "When we got off the ferry. And I said I was."

I was puzzled. "And you're not?"

Kate looked at me, her green eyes sad. She was try-ing to smile but it wasn't reaching her face.

"No," she said. "I'm not."

We sat there quietly for a few minutes, watching the people stroll up and down the walk, their sunburnt

faces glowing in the evening air. They looked comfortable, carefree, happy to be on an island off the coast of
southern California. Everything that, at that moment, I
was not.

"So what's wrong?" I finally asked.

Kate folded her arms across her chest, tugging at the
sleeves of her white cotton blouse. She turned to me,
but her eyes were just missing my face.

"Us, Noah," she said. "Us is what's wrong."

Any time a girl breaks up with you, it's painful. Always. But it may never be more painful than when you
hear it for the first time.

I leaned back into the stone bench. "What's wrong
with us?"

She looked away for a moment, biting down on her
bottom lip.

"I'm leaving next week," she said.

"I know. So?"

She turned back to me. "So what happens then?"

I shrugged. "You get on a plane and go to Princeton?"

She frowned, faint lines of irritation tying up around
her eyes. "Noah, you know what I'm talking about."

"No, I don't," I said. "We came over here to have dinner and spend the night at your family's place. Now
you're telling me there's a problem. Between us." I
paused. "Kate, I don't know what you're talking about."

She let out a sigh and shook her head. "Fine. I'm
going to the other side of the country. You're staying
here. How does that work?"

I shifted on the bench. "I don't know."

"I don't either," she said. "And that's the problem."

"That's a problem with location. Not with us."

She glanced at a group of junior high school kids ambling by, talking loudly and laughing. She looked back at me.

"We're eighteen," Kate said. "We're going in different directions."

Her words stung me. It didn't matter to me if they were true. They hurt. And I didn't like the feeling.

"Your mother write that speech for you?" I asked.

She rolled her eyes. "You know better."

"Sounds like her," I said. "All of a sudden, we aren't compatible because you're going to live in another state? That sounds exactly like her, Kate."

We sat there quietly for a few minutes. Her parents had been a sore spot during the entire year we'd been together. They didn't approve of their daughter dating someone who wasn't going to an Ivy League school and whose family was dysfunctional at best. I hadn't made it any easier by playing the surly, disaffected teen. We had put Kate in a difficult spot. And until that moment on Catalina, she'd always chosen me.

"Maybe it does sound like her," Kate finally said. "But maybe she's right, Noah."

"She's right about me, you mean."

"That's not what I meant and you know it," she said. "But is it realistic to think that we're gonna stay together over the next four years, three thousand miles apart?"

I turned and looked at her, her eyes tearing into the heart that she had created.

"I don't know," I said. "But I never thought we wouldn't try."

Her eyes fluttered, maybe surprised by what I said. She bit her bottom lip again. Tears formed at the corners of her eyes.

"Noah," she started, but choked up and stopped.

I looked away, my throat tightening.

She cleared her throat and tried again. "Noah, they won't . . ." Her voice trailed off.

The smell of popcorn wafted in the air from somewhere down the boardwalk. That same smell would forever evoke an unpleasant reaction in my gut.

"They won't what?" I asked, turning to her.

The tears were now rolling down her cheeks, dancing off her face and into her lap. She shook her head, her lips pressed together. The pain in her face answered my question.

"They won't let you go to Princeton," I said for her, "unless you cut me loose."

She nodded quickly, a sharp sob escaping from her mouth.

I leaned forward, resting my elbows on my knees, my brain numb. Her parents had played the toughest card. Me or her future. She'd tried to do it herself without laying the blame on her parents, trying to save me the embarrassment of being a black mark on her life.

"It's not fair," she mumbled.

"No, it's not," I said. "But that's your parents."

We sat there, not looking at one another for a while.

Over the years, I would come to realize that it was a no-brainer of a choice for too many reasons to run through. But at that moment, my second-place finish filled me with unfettered bitterness.

I stood up and shoved my hands into the pockets of my shorts. "You gotta go to Princeton."

"I don't have to," she said, trying to hold the sobs in her chest. "I could figure out another way to go, without their help."

We both knew that wasn't true, not at that point in our lives. And I knew, somewhere in my mind, that Kate wanted to go to Princeton. She wouldn't say it and I couldn't admit it, but even then, I think, I knew it was true.

"It's okay," I told her, turning to her. "You need to go."

She looked at me, the rims of her eyes red. "We don't have to tell them. We can still be together. Call each other, you can come visit, I'll see you when I come home."

I shrugged. "We can't hide from them forever. They'll know. They always do." I shook my head. "And what if they did find out? You come home for a break or something and they won't send you back." I shook my head again. "Not worth it, Kate."

She looked at me, frustrated, upset, knowing I was right. "I'm sorry," she said. "I just . . . I don't know what to do. I didn't know what to say to you."

My chest felt like it was being squeezed. "You said it fine. I get it."

"I'm sorry, Noah," she said, her tears spilling onto the concrete of the sidewalk.

"Me, too," I said.

I turned and headed up the walk. I heard her call behind me, probably wondering where I was going, since we'd planned to spend the night. But it was easy to lose her voice in the commotion of the evening revelers. I was heading to the dock to catch the last ferry. I didn't turn around because I couldn't look at her, couldn't spend one more minute with her if we couldn't be together the way I wanted to be together.

And she didn't come after me.

If I'd known that was the last time I'd see her alive, I would've turned around. Maybe I would've even taken on her parents. But I didn't know that. You can't ever know that. So I kept walking, hoping that the feeling in my chest that was squeezing tears out of my eyes would eventually go away.

 10

I opened the sliding screen door to my place just before one in the morning, the smell of jalapeños and nacho cheese immediately burning into my nostrils.

"Honey, you're home," Carter Hamm said from the sofa amidst a pile of beer cans, plastic wrap, and tortilla chips.

"How did you ever convince me to give you a key?" I asked, shutting the door behind me.

"I didn't," he said, wiggling his enormous frame into a sitting position. "I stole one."

"Ah."

He grinned, looking like a humongous Cheshire cat. "Ah."

Carter had played center to my small forward in high school, pulling guard to my fullback and juvenile delinquent to my better judgment. Despite our differences—the main one being that I thought the law should be obeyed and he thought the law was a pain in his ass—we had remained surfing buddies, occasional coworkers, and good friends.

He stretched out his legs, the bottom half of his six-foot-nine body unfurling like a damp straw wrapper. His bleached white hair glowed in the dark room, his black eyes shining against his tan skin. The white T-shirt said DO ME in big black letters, and long red shorts hung loosely to his knees. His size-sixteen feet were bare, his sandals most likely buried somewhere beneath the tornado of crap he had created on my sofa.

He lifted a paper plate in my direction. "Nachos?"

"No thanks," I said, tossing my keys on the kitchen counter. I walked to the fridge, pulled out a Red Trolley, ripped the cap off, and drank half of it.

Carter let out a low whistle. "Dude, if I had known we were gonna be drinking, I would've waited for you."

"We're not drinking," I mumbled, staring out the back door. The whitecaps in the ocean did nosedives under the moonlight.

I felt Carter's eyes on my back. "You alright?"

"No, not really."

"Gonna tell me?"

"Not now."

"Cool. You wanna hit the water?"

I watched the ocean shiver and shake a hundred yards away, empty and navy blue in the dark. I knew that some time on my board trying to decipher and outsmart the waves might temporarily salve my wounds.

I finished the beer and set the empty bottle on the counter.

I turned to Carter. "Let's go."

There is something mystical about surfing between the darkness of the ocean and the glow of the evening moonlight. It isn't just that you feel dwarfed by the planet in the quiet of the night, but more like you have found the edge of the world and could dive off if you wanted to.

That edge was where I learned to hide when I was growing up.

When I was nine years old, a family down the street was moving out of town and they gave me an eight-foot board that was dinged up and otherwise headed for the trash. I took it down to Mission Bay that afternoon and spent three hours learning to stand on it in the calm, flat water. The next afternoon I took the bus down to Law Street and watched the locals tear up the waves, sucking in their movements and committing to memory how they maneuvered their boards so easily through the water. I waited until about sunset, when everyone else had gone, and paddled out.

On the ninth try, I managed to get myself up long enough to feel like a surfer.

After that ninth try in my ninth year, the ocean became my real home, much calmer than the house in Bay Park. There was no drunken mother passed out on the shoreline, no unknown father haunting me below the surface of the water. I grew up on three-foot, left-breaking sets that you could bounce all the way in to the shore.

The ocean and its waves raised me and I was better for it.

Carter and I rode for forty-five minutes, carving our boards into the black mass of the waves as they rhythmically approached and then left us. In the quiet darkness, the noise of the boards cutting the water was magnified, like the sound of two large hands rubbing together.

We were straddling our boards out beyond the break. People who don't surf tend to look at this act as some sort of Zen-like activity that surfers do, trying to become one with the ocean or something like that. In actuality, we sit on our boards because we are too exhausted to paddle in.

"So," Carter said, running his hands through his soaked hair. "You gonna tell me what the problemo is?"

He looked like a giant buoy sticking straight out of the ocean.

I wiped the water from my eyes. "Remember Kate Crier?"

He pretended to think about it. "Vaguely. She was that girl that you wasted an entire year on, dumped your ass right before she left for college because her parents thought you were trash, and you've pined intermittently for over the years." He paused. "Yeah, Noah. I remember Kate."

"I found her today. Dead."

He cupped his hands, dipped them into the water, and brought them up to his mouth. Carter is the only human I've ever run across who enjoys the taste of saltwater. He swished the water around for a moment like it was mouthwash, then spit it onto his board.

"Well, that's not so hot," he said.

I glanced at the dots of light along the shore. "No."

"You found her?"

I detailed Marilyn's visit and how I had come upon Kate.

Carter nodded in the dark, his enormous head moving slowly against the backdrop of the moon. "I'm sorry."

I shrugged, listening to the waves die up ahead of us. "Her dad wants me to find out what happened."

"Same guy that banned your car from his driveway because it looked like it might leak oil?"

"Same guy."

Carter snorted. "I hope you told him to fornicate solo."

I chuckled softly, shaking my head.

"But of course you didn't," Carter said, knowing the answer.

I leaned back on the board, my head floating on the surface of the water. The sky looked like a black piece of crepe paper that had been poked with several needles, bright beacons of light streaming through the holes. I hadn't seen Kate in over eleven years, but now I felt as if a piece of me had disappeared.

"Well, at least they've got money," Carter mumbled, patting the top of the water with his baseball glove–like hands. "So we know we'll get paid."

"We?" I asked.

He leaned forward and flattened himself onto his board, his long arms looking like small windmills as he began to paddle away. "Well, hell, I can't have you sulking like one of my ex-girlfriends until you figure it out. I'll be Hutch to your Starsky."

I sat up and smiled. "Awesome."

"Yeah, I am," he said over his shoulder as he moved toward the shore. "Plus, Kate was my friend too at one time."

I nodded to myself and wished that she were still alive to hear Carter say that.

 *12*

I crawled out of bed early after our late-night surfing expedition, nursed my small hangover with a glass of orange juice, and headed out in the early morning traffic.

I took I-5 up to the eastern edge of La Jolla and then went east on Highway 52, a concrete artery that bisected San Diego County through the narrow, brush-lined canyons of University City and Clairemont Mesa. The highway had been nothing more than a dirt valley when I was growing up, but as people moved farther and farther to the east in order to still call San Diego home, the 52 became the newest freeway to connect the outer reaches of the county to the coast.

The medical examiner's office was out in the wasteland of business parks known as Kearney Mesa. A triangular area surrounded by three different freeways, the region had slowly transformed itself over a period of about ten years from dusty vacant lots to low-slung white and gray buildings that housed every conceivable type of industry and business. It was nearly the geographical heart of San Diego, but seemed devoid of life or character.

The ME's building was off Ruffin Road, and I parked in the lot out front. The office smelled like lemon, and I wrinkled my nose as the glass doors swung closed behind me. The area was small and compact—a chest-high counter, two desks, couple of filing cabinets, a radio on top of a television and VCR in the corner. A hallway disappeared off the back of the windowless room.

I rang the metal bell on the desk and fifteen seconds later James Minton emerged from the back hall and made a face like I'd forgotten to put pants on.

"Fuck you want, Braddock?" he asked, his voice a mixture of gravel and whine.

"Good to see you, too, James."

The face remained. "No it ain't. What the fuck you want?" He held up his pudgy hand before I could respond. "Know what? Don't care what you want. Go away."

I laughed. "I've missed you."

His hand shrank to a middle finger.

Minton was medium height, with a gut that was anything but medium. He had on a white coat over a pair of jeans and a black T-shirt that barely contained his girth. A thin dark mustache snaked over his upper lip. The dark hair on his head was thinning, a fact he tried to cover up by buzzing it short. Dark gray eyes stared me down.

"I'm serious," he said. "I don't have time for you. Go away."

"Can't."

"Door's right behind you. Turn around and put one foot in front of the other. You'll get it."

I looked over the counter at him. "Why so bitter?"

He folded his arms across his chest, reminding me of a fat, angry Buddha. "Last time I saw you, I found you in the back, having moved a body and copying some records. Then that big asshole that follows you around picked me up and pinned me in the corner of the room until you were done." He pointed a finger at me. "You fucked the whole thing up."

"You didn't answer the bell and I was trying to do my job."

He waved a hand in the air, beads of sweat appearing on his forehead. "Whatever, Braddock. You pissed me off and I don't like to be pissed off."

I smiled. "Me either. But I'm not leaving."

Minton stared at me for a moment, then rolled his eyes. "Two minutes."

I nodded. "You get a DB last night?"

He pulled a clipboard off the wall behind him, looked at it for a moment, then nodded. "Yep."

"Kate Crier?"

Minton looked again, then back at me. "Yep."

"Cause of death?"

"Still to be determined." He glanced at the clock on the wall. "One minute left."

"Looked like strangulation from what I saw," I said.

His left eye twitched. "Maybe."

"Maybe?"

He gave a small shrug. "Couple other things I need to look at."

"Like?"

Minton thought about it for a moment, then looked at the clock again. "Like your two minutes are up."

"That wasn't two minutes," I protested.

"Was in my world."

I didn't want to push it because if I was going to learn anything about Kate's death, I would need his help. I pulled a card from my wallet and placed it on the counter. "I'd appreciate a call when you know more."

"Well, hell," he said, raising his eyebrows. "I'll get right on that, Mr. Private Dick. Emphasis on Dick. Just for you."

I smiled. "Got two tickets behind the plate for Friday's game. Dodgers are in town." I opened the door to the hallway. Minton was the biggest baseball fan I knew. Great seats were his weakness. "Yours, if I get a call by the end of the day."

He muttered something under his breath.

I turned around. "What?"

His mouth curled into a disgusted frown, most likely due to the fact that I knew he would never turn down great seats.

"I said," Minton replied, spinning on his heel and heading toward the back hall, "fuck off."

 *13*

Minton's statement about a "couple of other things" rang in my ears as I walked back to my car. I tried to remember what else I'd seen when I'd opened the trunk of the car, but the only thing I could recall with any clarity was Kate's face. I knew there would be no shaking that.

I was pondering that thought when I saw a guy sitting on the hood of my Jeep. He was twirling my radio antenna like a baton, watching it very closely as if he wanted to perfect the move. Another guy was leaning against the white Lexus parked next to the Jeep, watching him.

The guy with the antenna looked up. "You Braddock?"

"No," I said. "Me Tarzan."

He dropped the antenna on the asphalt and looked at his partner. "Funny, you think?"

His partner rotated his head in my direction, squinting into the morning sunlight. "Very."

The guy on the Jeep slid off the hood and tilted his head to one side, cracking his neck. He was about my height, with a square head and more fat than muscle. His face was dotted by acne scars, heavier around the chin. His black hair was slicked back off his forehead, so tight it looked like it hurt. He wore a white tank top, black cotton sweats, and construction boots.

He looked again at his partner. "So. We gonna do this, Ramon, or what?"

Ramon was shorter and dressed a hell of a lot better. He wore a gray silk shirt and black linen slacks, expensive leather huaraches on his feet. His black hair was cut short, long sideburns creeping down his cheeks. A gold hoop dangled fashionably from his left ear. His eyes were flat and cold, like steel.

He held out a hand to his partner. "Easy, Manny."

"Yeah, Manny. Easy," I said.

Manny scowled, and I doubted that anything came easy for him.

Ramon looked at me. "Can I ask why you are here, Mr. Braddock? Visiting the medical examiner?" He spoke softly with a heavy Hispanic accent.

"You can ask. Sure."

Ramon eyed me for a moment, then a small smile crept onto his lips. "But you won't answer?"

I shook my head and wrinkled my nose. "Don't really feel compelled." I looked at Manny. "Sorry. Big word. *Compelled* means 'gotta.' "

Manny continued to scowl. "Dude, you are not funny."

"Guys," I said, preparing for the confrontation. "Sorry, but I can't hang out with you anymore. Things to do, places to be, you know the deal."

Manny stepped in front of my car door and smiled.

I returned the smile. "In about ten seconds, Manny, you are gonna wish you had chosen breakfast instead of me this morning." I looked at Ramon. "Unless you have any more questions, I'm going to kick his ass."

Ramon shrugged, then nodded at Manny. Manny lurched at me and swung. I stepped inside the swing and thrust my right palm up under his chin. His teeth cracked together, his eyes slammed shut, and he took a step back. I moved to the side, lifted my leg up, and jammed my foot into the side of Manny's knee. A muffled scream emerged from the broken teeth and blood in his mouth as he crumpled to the ground.

I stepped back and looked at Ramon. "You next?"

He didn't look impressed, which concerned me. He cocked his head to the side. "Mr. Braddock. Do you know the name Alejandro Costilla?"

I watched Manny curl into a tight ball on the sidewalk. Alejandro Costilla. My life had suddenly become a lot more complicated.

I looked back at Ramon, trying not to show him anything. "No."

Ramon let the same small smile I'd seen earlier crawl back on his lips. "You are a liar, Mr. Braddock."

I picked up my antenna and got into the Jeep, the window already rolled down. "I've been called worse."

Ramon nodded, shoved his hands in the pockets of his expensive pants, and leaned in the window, so his eyes were at the same level as mine. "Yes, I think you are a liar, Mr. Braddock. But that is your choice." He turned to Manny and offered him a hand, but Manny was busy hugging his knee to his chest and bellowing in pain. Ramon shrugged and looked back at me. "I believe Mr. Costilla will have an interest in speaking to you about your visit this morning." He winked. "So I'm sure I will see you again. Soon."

I drove off before he could really scare the crap out of me.

 *14*

"Did you use your Jew Kung Fu?"

Carter was stretched out on one of the deck chairs on my patio, a pair of sunglasses and blue board shorts the only things on his body impeding the rays of the sun. I sat in the chair next to him, recounting my morning, as we watched the sunbathers and tourists stroll by on the boardwalk.

"It's called Krav Maga, moron," I replied, irritated by his political incorrectness.

A half-eaten apple rested in his right hand. He waved it in my direction. "Whatever. Did you use it?"

I'd learned Krav Maga from a guy in college in exchange for a six pack and help with a lit paper. I asked him to teach me because I thought it was cool. I didn't know that it would end up being a highlight on my resume.

"Yeah, I used it. The one guy wasn't there to fight and the other dude wasn't a problem," I told him. "That said, there actually is a big problem."

Carter sat up in his chair, lifted his sunglasses above his eyes, and let loose an earsplitting whistle that brought the pedestrian traffic on the walk to a halt. He pointed at a woman in a red bikini on rollerblades. "You are hot."

When her look of alarm disappeared, she gave him a shy grin and continued on her way.

Carter turned to me, dropping the glasses back into place. "Big problem?"

I shaded my eyes against the sunlight. "Alejandro Costilla."

Carter stopped in mid-bite and lowered the piece of fruit. "Come again?"

"The guys that were waiting on me," I explained. "Costilla sent them."

He stared at me for a moment, looked at the apple like it contained poison, then back at me. "Tell me you're screwing with me, Noah."

"Can't. Wish I could, but I can't."

Carter fell onto his back and dropped the apple onto his bare stomach. "And you dropped one of his dudes?"

"Uh, yep."

He adjusted the mirrored Oakleys that covered his eyes. "Well. Fuck me."

"I know."

I watched two teenagers at the shoreline strap on their leashes, pick up their boards, and run into the water, gliding the noses of their boards into the waves as they made their way out to the lineup.

I wanted to chase after them and forget about the new complications in my life. But I knew it wasn't gonna happen at that moment.

Carter propped himself up on his elbows. "What the hell do they want with you?"

"Don't know," I answered. "They were waiting for me when I left the ME's. Said that was where Mr. Costilla's interest was."

"With Kate?"

I nodded. "I guess."

He picked up the apple and finished it methodically. He wiped his mouth with the palm of his hand, then looked at me. "What the hell was she into?"

It was the same question that had been dancing in my mind since I'd left them. They clearly knew why I went to see Minton. "They know about Kate's death. Why does it matter to them?"

"I don't remember Kate doing drugs," Carter said.

"I don't remember anyone we knew doing the kind of drugs it would take to draw Costilla's attention," I said.

Carter sat all the way up. He faced straight ahead at the tourists, the beach, and the water, but the sunglasses made it impossible for me to tell where his focus was.

"I don't like this, Noah," he said, finally, shaking his head slowly. "Costilla . . . we don't want to get near him."

I agreed with him, but didn't know how to get out of it. "Unfortunately, that's gonna be impossible to avoid now."

He nodded slowly. "Yeah."

"And I think the longer we wait, the worse it might get."

Carter nodded again.

"Can you set up a meeting?" I asked, knowing that, with his connections, he could.

Carter lifted the sunglasses up and rested them on top of his head, the black of the frames contrasting with his white hair and bronze face. He cocked his head to the side, one eye open, the other closed. "Yeah. If you really want me to, I will." He paused. "But you better be sure on this."

Reluctance wasn't something I was used to hearing in his voice, and that bothered me. Normally, he carried enough confidence for the both of us. And most of the rest of the human population, too.

"I think we have to," I said.

He kept the one open eye on me. "Noah, if they're interested in Kate, there's a reason. Costilla doesn't fuck around. And most likely, whatever the reason, you're not gonna like it. Neither are her asshole parents." He paused. "That gonna be something you can deal with?"

Two seagulls buzzed over the patio and out toward the water, chirping like angry lovers. Sitting on the patio, watching the waves, almost always felt cathartic, relaxing. Now, that feeling had turned to fear.

"We'll see," I told him. "We'll see."

 *15*

Carter had been gone for about an hour, leaving without a word, presumably to set up our meeting with Costilla. I was contemplating what I might say to one of the most powerful druglords known to man when the phone mercifully interrupted my efforts.

"Braddock." Minton sounded irritated.

"That's me."

"I want the tickets delivered to the office by five tonight."

"Done."

"And if they are anything less than exquisite seats, you can feel free to never set foot in my office again."

I thought of about five great things to say about his use of the word "exquisite," but I reminded myself that I needed his help and held my tongue. "They're great seats, I promise."

"Death was caused by strangulation," Minton said

quickly. "Probably about twelve hours before you found her."

Not a big surprise. I'd figured that out on my own.

"No other trauma to the body that contributed to the death," Minton continued.

"No other bumps or bruises?" I asked.

"None," he answered. "But the tox screen was loaded."

I took a deep breath. "Loaded?"

"Heroin," Minton said. "And some alcohol."

I tried to process that. "Could she have overdosed?"

"Nope," Minton said confidently. "Her windpipe was crushed. Lots of residual, which says to me she was an addict. She had a decent amount in her system, but my guess would be that was a regular thing. The screen showed long-term use, not a binge that would've killed her."

His words felt like a hammer hitting me in the spine. The thought of Kate using drugs felt as foreign to me as her being dead.

"Needle marks?" I asked.

"Nothing fresh, but there was some scarring on the left arm and in between the toes." Minton paused. "She wasn't a recreational user. It was a way of life for this girl."

My brain spun like a tornado. "You're sure?"

"Positive," he said. "And, Braddock? We didn't have this conversation. I haven't even filled out the report yet."

"Got it."

"Tickets by five," he said and hung up.

I set the phone down and tried to picture Kate as a drug addict. We'd smoked a little pot in high school, but mainly for experimentation and fun. Neither of us had much of a taste for it. We drank our share, but stayed away from anything that got snorted or injected. I couldn't imagine Kate being involved in anything worse than that.

But Minton clearly disagreed with my imagination.

Randall Tower hadn't mentioned any drug use to me. It wouldn't be surprising if he didn't know, though. Most people try to hide their bad habits from the ones they love, but rich people turned it into an art.

I pondered that as I called my buddy with the baseball tickets and arranged to have them delivered to Minton. He'd confused the hell out of me, but he'd earned them.

The front door opened, and Carter filled the space.

"We're on," he said, his face expressionless.

"When?"

Carter stepped aside, and Ramon, the nattily dressed thug from earlier in the day, stood beside him.

Ramon smiled and pointed a nasty-looking pistol at my gut. "Now."

 *16*

A ride to the South Bay wasn't what I had in mind for the afternoon, but when an internationally wanted drug kingpin agrees to meet with you and sends his people to escort you, a sandwich and a nap place a distant second.

Carter and I rode in the back of a dark blue Cadillac, Ramon in the front passenger seat with another man driving. The other man hadn't gotten out of the car, and all that I could see was a black handlebar mustache sticking off the side his face, his head the size of a watermelon.

We drove south on the five, past Lindbergh Field, the ancient El Cortez Hotel, and Balboa Park, home to most of San Diego's cultural activities. We moved by the on-ramp to the Coronado Bridge and then through the industrial grounds of National City and Imperial Beach to the last U.S. exit in San Ysidro.

There are three reasons to take the San Ysidro exit.

You can park and walk across the border into Tijuana, like the thousands of tourists that do just that every day. You can get off the freeway and head back to where you came from, avoiding the dangerous streets of one of Baja California's poorest cities. Or you can go shopping at the only outlet mall located at a United States international border.

The Cadillac turned into the parking lot of the outlets and drove to the western end of the strip mall.

"Guys, if we could hit the Mikasa store, that would be great," I said. "I need some new goblets."

"Just a word of warning," Ramon said, not bothering to turn around. "Mr. Costilla does not find many things funny."

I closed my big trap.

The car came to a stop at the end of the lot, idling next to the curb.

Ramon turned around. "I'm going to assume that you know that just because you don't see any guns doesn't mean there aren't any guns." He smiled. "Follow me, please."

Carter and I slid out of the backseat. The driver stayed in the car and U-turned the Cadillac into a handicapped space.

We walked with Ramon past the Nike store, moving with the crowd of shoppers, a mix of local Mexicans and tourists looking for bargains. At the end of the row of shops, Ramon stopped in front of an empty suite. He produced a key and unlocked the door, holding it open for us. "After you."

The front of the store was vacant, apparently in the process of being renovated. Paint cans and their lids were strewn across the concrete floor, with several ladders pushed up against the walls.

Ramon shut the door behind us. "The back room," he said, pointing toward the door at the rear of the space.

I looked at Carter, who shrugged and nodded in that direction. We walked to the back and stopped in front of a partially closed door. If the shop were open for business, it would've been to the back office or the storeroom. For us, I wasn't quite sure where it would lead.

Ramon yelled out something in Spanish.

"Come in," a voice said from behind the door.

We went in. The storage room was double the size of the storefront, all gray concrete and cinder blocks. Empty metal shelves lined the walls from floor to ceiling.

One man stood near the back door on the far side of the room, an Uzi resting in his large hands and pointed in our direction.

Alejandro Costilla paced back and forth between us in the middle of the room, an angry cat in a human body.

He was taller than I expected, probably six foot two, his athletic frame moving effortlessly in gray slacks, a white silk shirt, and black leather sandals. His head was shaved clean, a tan, gleaming scalp in place of hair. A thick black goatee made its way around his mouth. His eyes were narrow slits, outlined by thin black brows.

He froze when he saw us, as if we'd interrupted his concentration. His eyes narrowed a little more. He pointed at me. "You're Braddock?"

His voice was high pitched for a man and it stopped me for a moment. He sounded like Charlie Brown.

"Yeah," I said, regaining my composure.

He glared at Carter. "And you're the one that set this up with Ramon?"

Carter nodded slightly. I realized his eyes were focused on the guy with the gun.

"He said you can be trusted," Costilla said.

"That's half right," Carter told him.

Costilla raised an eyebrow. "What's the other half?"

"Feared, too," Carter replied, expressionless.

Costilla stared at him for a moment before letting his mouth slide into a thin smile.

"Perhaps Ramon said that, too."

Carter shrugged.

Costilla started pacing again, but kept an eye on me. "You are investigating the murder?"

"I am," I said, trying to relax. "You knew her?"

"We'd met," he said, rubbing his hands together.

"In San Francisco?"

He waved a hand in the air, the silver rings on his fingers flashing like lightning. "I don't remember and it doesn't matter." He stopped moving for a moment and turned his full gaze on me. "What do you know so far?"

I thought about that for a moment. I knew several things, but I wasn't sure how wise it would be to share those things with Costilla. I needed to know what he wanted.

"I know she's dead," I said.

He stared at me for a moment, his eyes like black holes. He put his hands in his pockets.

"What do you know?" he asked quietly.

"Why?"

He shook his head slightly and looked at the floor, as if I were a child that kept making the same mistake. "Because I want to know."

It was a statement made by a man who was not used to being questioned. And it chilled the room.

"I know I found her in the trunk of the car," I said, deciding to play it semi-straight. "I know I think she was strangled. I know the medical examiner is still working on it. And I know her parents asked me to look into her death."

Costilla looked up and clapped his hands together softly, mockingly. "That's better."

I glanced at Carter out of the corner of my eye. He was still locked in a staredown with Costilla's bodyguard.

"That last part," Costilla said to me. "You are done looking into her death."

"I am?"

Costilla nodded, quick and hard. "You are."

"Normally the people that hire me tell me when I'm done," I said. "You didn't hire me."

Costilla placed his hands in his pockets. "No, I didn't. But I am telling you that you are done."

"And if I say I'm not?" I asked, watching him. My spine felt like an aluminum bat, the tension locking me up completely.

He started pacing again, this time not looking at me. "You will be well compensated for your time, Mr. Braddock."

I watched him walk, confident and assured.

"Why do you want me off?" I asked.

He stopped and turned to me, an amused look on his face. "You ask a lot of questions, man. Stay with me for a second, but you do know who I am, right?"

I nodded.

He smiled, exposing bright, white teeth. "Of course you do. I ask that question to demonstrate something. Do you understand?"

"Not sure."

"My point is you shouldn't be asking questions of me," he said, his smile growing wider. "Instead, you should be thinking about how to make sure I don't fucking kill you today."

I knew that, but I also knew that if I bowed down to this guy, I was done forever.

"I don't always do the right thing," I told him.

He nodded, evidently agreeing. "I heard that. But doing the wrong thing and doing something completely *loco* are two different things." He nailed me with his eyes. "And right now you are on the *loco* side."

I watched the lines around his eyes intensify.

"Don't know what to tell you," I said.

"There are two responses for you to choose from," he said, holding up two fingers. "Yes, I'm going to back off. Or no, I'm staying on it." He waggled the two fingers. "Simple choice. I will let you make the decision. But you only get one chance."

I paused, considering where my answer might take me. I knew what the right thing to say was, the safe thing. I knew which answer would get us out of the empty room and away from Costilla. But I couldn't get it out of my mouth.

"No," I said. "I'm staying on it."

I heard Carter clear his throat.

Costilla folded his arms across his chest. "An unfortunate decision," he said, his eyes burning holes into me. "Ricardo will see you out. The back door."

"I don't think so," Carter said.

Costilla glared at him. "Too bad." He snapped his fingers. "Ricardo."

Ricardo waved the gun, motioning for us to move.

Carter finally moved his eyes from Ricardo to Costilla. "An unfortunate decision."

Costilla returned the stare but said nothing.

I felt a knot form in my stomach and followed Carter toward the door. I knew Carter wouldn't be moving unless he had a plan. Now I just needed to get inside his head and figure out what it was before we both took bullets to the back of the head.

Ricardo got to the door and opened it with his right hand, holding the gun in his left.

Then Ricardo's head exploded.

Bullets poured into the room, ricocheting off the walls like marbles in an ice cooler. I dove to the floor, Carter landing next to me. I heard some yelling in Spanish from the storefront. I rolled next to the wall and looked at Carter.

He grinned back at me.

I heard some more yelling in Spanish, the voices retreating from the room. The bullets finally settled down, the silence nearly louder than the violence. The stench of hot metal and smoke filled my nose and stung my eyes.

"Carter?" a voice asked above us.

"It's clear," another voice said.

We both sat up.

Timmy and Jimmy Tate stood in the doorway, each holding something that looked like an AK-47.

Jimmy nodded at me. "What's up, Noah?"

The Tates were identical twins. They were buddies of Carter's. Working buddies. Psychotic buddies. Painfully thin, with pale, white skin, they both stood about five foot eight. Sad eyes and monobrows made them look like forlorn raccoons. Each sported a tight Marine crew cut of jet-black hair. Timmy wore a white bandana around his forehead. Jimmy sported a green one. Camouflage pants and a couple of black T-shirts completed their renegade ensemble.

The only way to tell them apart was that Jimmy's right eye was fake, the result of taking a pool cue in the face during a fight with his brother. He'd somehow obtained a glass eye that had a red stone in the middle of it, giving him the look of having stepped out of a photograph where the flash didn't work correctly.

That's how I knew it was Jimmy that was talking to me.

I looked around, scanning the room. "Where's Costilla?"

"Beat it out the door," Timmy said. "Think I got somebody in the shoulder, though."

I turned back around to them. "What are you doing here?"

They nodded at Carter.

Carter stared at me like I was a moron. "You think we were gonna come in here naked?"

"Gotta go," Jimmy said, backing out the door.

"Yep," Timmy said, following him.

"Call you guys," Carter said. "Thanks."

They disappeared out the door.

"The twins have the right idea. Let's get the hell out of here," Carter said.

I stood and stepped over Ricardo's bullet-ridden body, the blood pooling in splotches around what was left of his head.

I looked back at the door that Alejandro Costilla had escaped through, possibly wounded by someone he would associate with me.

I knew he wouldn't wait long to track me down.

 *17*

Carter's car, if that's what you'd call it, waited for us at the far end of the parking lot. He'd arranged for the Tate brothers to deliver the beast.

Carter owned a 1985 Dodge Ram Charger, a monstrosity of an automobile that sat high off the ground on tires the size of carousels. He had cut the top off because he decided it was easier to throw his surfboards in that way. The seats were torn in different spots, the yellow foam oozing out from beneath the duct tape he'd used to try to cover up the tears.

The 4x4 had originally been painted bright red, but Carter is anything but bright red. So he'd painted it all black, then added white stripes on the sides and back. Sort of a zebra hybrid look. Save for the giant skull and crossbones he'd stenciled on the hood.

Carter's car.

We drove without talking, the wind slapping around us loudly and urgently as we made our way up the freeway, before exiting and taking the bridges over the southern edge of Mission Bay, past the Bahia Resort Hotel and onto the small isthmus of land between the bay and the ocean that was Mission Beach.

I wasn't as worried as I should have been about Costilla. I wanted to be anxious, to be nervous, but I couldn't stop thinking about Kate and where her life had taken her. I figured the panic would set in later. Like when I found Costilla waiting for me in my house or something.

Carter pulled to a halt in front of my place, but the motor under the skull kept humming.

"You could've told him you'd drop it," he said.

I nodded. "Could've."

"Didn't figure you would, though."

I opened the door and dropped to the ground, my chin barely over the seat cushion. "You are a think tank."

He ran a hand through his bleached hair. "Want my thoughts?"

"No."

He gave them to me anyway. "She was dealing or she was a mule. Why else would she have had contact with Costilla? You don't buy just a weekend's worth from him."

I smoothed a piece of duct tape on the seat. The same thought had crossed my mind, but I couldn't get it to work for me. I couldn't picture any thirty-year-old woman from a filthy rich background operating in the heroin trade, and I couldn't even begin to think that Kate could've been involved in something that dark.

Carter gripped the steering wheel. A giant in his giant car. "So she either had her own business going or she delivered for him."

"Neither makes sense," I told him.

"We're not trying to make sense. We're trying to make a connection." He stepped on the accelerator, the engine revving like a jet plane. "Gotta go. Got some things to do."

With Carter, it's hard to tell. He could've meant grocery shopping or he could've meant hunting down Costilla.

I didn't ask.

"Okay," I said, stepping back and shutting the door. "The service for Kate is tomorrow."

He nodded. "I never miss a party."

"Not much of a party."

He nodded again, stepped on the gas, and peeled out in the alley, smoke trailing behind him as he disappeared.

I went inside my house, more cautious than usual. After I checked in the closets, under the bed, and in the freezer, I settled out on the patio with a beer under the late afternoon sun, watching a few stragglers on the water try to make something of waves that were amounting to nothing.

In college, I had developed an affection for late afternoons on the water. Between my classes during the day and waiting tables at night, it was the one part of the day that I had free to surf. The waves were usually awful, but it never bothered me much. The professors and the restaurant customers couldn't touch me out there, and I used that time to enjoy myself and keep my head clear.

I sipped at the beer, thinking about how Kate could've been connected to Costilla. It became a pointless exercise because I realized I probably didn't really know Kate anymore. The girl I remembered was gone the second I left Catalina Island, and she had vanished somewhere along the way in the years since I had last seen her.

"Some things never change," a voice said from behind me.

"I don't think I ever gave you a key, Liz," I said, without turning around.

Detective Liz Santangelo came around and sat on the patio wall, her back to the sun and sea. "You didn't. Door was open."

"I'm so careless."

"Might want to change that," she said, folding her arms across her black blouse and crossing her legs, the white cotton of the capri pants wrinkling at the knees.

I looked past her down to the shoreline. The waves were small and slow, and I knew I wasn't missing anything out there, as the stragglers gave up and looked back at the water, shaking their heads, wishing for better things from the ocean.

"Yesterday," I said finally. "I shouldn't have said what I said."

"No, you shouldn't have," she replied.

I knew that Liz took enough grief from her colleagues about being a woman in a man's job. I didn't need to make it tougher for her. I'd been pissed off and out of line.

"So I'm sorry," I said. "Really."

She nodded. "Thanks."

The ocean hitting the shore filled the silence between us. I thought maybe she was surprised at my apology, but I wasn't sure.

"Were you down at the border earlier today?" she asked.

I drank some more of the beer and squinted at her. "Not that I recall."

She tilted her head to the left, her eyes narrowing a bit. "Little shoot-out down there this afternoon. Alejandro Costilla and a few of his friends were seen fleeing. One guy dead. Two other guys were seen leaving the outlets."

"I've never cared for outlet shopping. Seems like cheating. Dangerous, too, apparently."

"Witness says they left in a convertible. A big, God-awful-looking convertible."

I shook my head. "Convertibles are tough on my hair, Liz. And you know how vain I can be."

She watched me for a moment. I stared back. I was actually staring over her shoulder, watching two seagulls battle for a hot dog bun in midair, but I didn't tell her that.

"What the fuck are you doing messing around with Alejandro Costilla?" she finally asked.

"I would have to be an idiot to be messing around with Alejandro Costilla," I said. "Detective."

She nodded in agreement. "Yeah. You would have to be an idiot. And most of the time you are."

I finished the beer and pointed the empty bottle at her. "That was rude. After I apologized and everything. I think you should leave now."

She stood and sighed deeply, her annoyance with me evident. It was a sigh I'd gotten used to hearing when we'd been together.

"This is bigger than you, Noah," she said, her voice softening. "Trust me."

"Trust you?" I said. "What's bigger than me? Tell me what I don't know."

"I can't," she said, shaking her head.

"Then if you can't trust me, why would I trust you?"

"Because I'm telling you to."

The fact that she wouldn't tell me what she knew bothered me more than her attitude. Our relationship had always been rocky, personally and professionally, but we'd always been straight with one another. Our paths had crossed professionally over the last couple of years, and while we weren't best friends, she'd never asked me to get out of the way.

"That's not enough, Liz, and you know it," I said. "You knew it before you said it."

She looked at me for a moment, and I thought

maybe she was going to tell me what I was missing. But it passed quickly, replaced by an expression that said she knew better than I did.

"Noah, whatever you're doing," she told me, walking by me toward the house, "don't. Because as good as you think you are, Costilla is better at being bad. Much better."

I heard the front door close. One of the seagulls gave up the fight for the bun, flew toward me, and landed on the wall, his beady eyes bearing down on me.

No one was on my side.

 *18*

Kate's service wasn't that different from other funerals that I'd been to. All Hallows Catholic Church sits atop Mount Soledad, overlooking the La Jolla shoreline, but even the view couldn't change why we were there. Lots of flowers and crying, and everyone wishing they were someplace else.

The one exception was that her husband threatened to rip my head off.

The service had ended, and Carter and I were out in the courtyard next to the church, watching the Criers receive condolences from friends and family. I hadn't wanted to come. Not that anyone ever wants to attend a funeral, but Kate's death felt too close. I wasn't ready to bury her. But I realized that if I was going to figure out what had happened to her, I was going to have to get used to doing things I wasn't ready to do.

"They look wrecked," Carter said, watching Marilyn and Ken nod and shake hands.

"Yeah."

"You gonna talk to them?"

I shook my head. "Not here. They've got enough to deal with today."

Carter nodded in agreement. "Yeah. I don't think Marilyn would care to see me anyway."

I thought about that for a moment. "Was the last time you saw her . . ."

"Yep."

"The whole I-jump-farther—"

"—if-I'm-naked episode," Carter confirmed.

The week before Kate and I broke up, Kate's older sister, Emily, was home from UCLA with some friends having a party. The UCLA coeds had immediately taken to Carter, and he'd responded in kind. They'd dared him to jump off the roof of the Criers' house into the pool. He'd claimed he could only do it naked because he jumped farther without any clothes on.

Unfortunately, Marilyn Crier had walked out onto the patio just in time to see Carter soar over her into her pool. Naked.

"An unforgettable performance," I said.

"Legendary," he said. Then he tilted his head. "Hey. Didn't you and Emily—"

"Shut up," I said, cutting him off.

Almost as if she'd heard us, Emily Crier emerged from a group of people near her parents and came toward us.

"Noah," she said, a tired smile forcing its way onto her face. "It's good to see you."

We hugged briefly, and I was surprised by how little she'd changed. Slightly taller than Kate, she was still model thin. Her blond hair looked yellow in the sunlight, cut slightly above her shoulders. Soft brown eyes. She wore a black sundress with expensive-looking black heels. Put a bikini on her and she could've been back cheering for Carter in the pool that night.

She put a hand on Carter's arm. "You are still . . . huge."

Normally, he would have had at least fourteen responses to that statement, most of them obnoxious and funny. But maybe the most startling thing about Carter could be his sense of civility.

He nodded. "Good to see you, Em."

She returned the nod, and an awkward pause engulfed the three of us like a bubble.

"I'm sorry, Emily," I said finally. "I really am."

"Thank you," she said, shading her eyes from the sun. "It's . . . I don't know."

She looked around the courtyard for a moment, watching her parents shake more hands. She kept snapping the fingers of her left hand softly, trying to burn the nervous uncomfortable energy that comes from losing someone close to you.

She turned back to me. "Dad hired you, I hear."

"He did. After your mother hired me."

She laughed and shook her head. "That is a partnership I never would've bet on."

I watched her father, forcing a smile as he hugged an older woman. "Me either."

"Was Mom a complete bitch to you?"

"Not complete. Partial, maybe."

She groaned. "I doubt that."

"Which one's Randall?" Carter asked, scanning the crowd.

Emily spotted Kate's husband first. "Over there. Tall, handsome." She paused and the finger snapping came to a halt. "Huge bastard."

I recognized Randall speaking with two other men.

"He's not so tall," Carter observed.

"Bastard?" I asked, surprised by Emily's comment. "You don't like your brother-in-law?"

Her stare was still locked on Randall. "Have you met him?"

"Yeah."

"What did you think?"

I glanced at Carter, but he was looking at Randall, too. "Seemed alright."

Emily turned to me, the soft brown eyes now hard as slate. "He's a prick, Noah."

Her face flushed, her anger gathering itself. "Phony two-faced prick. He didn't love Kate."

"How do you know?"

She turned back in Randall's direction. "He was cheating on her. From day one."

I looked across the courtyard at Randall. I hadn't pegged him for infidelity when we'd met. I thought there was something off about him, but I didn't get the sense that he didn't love Kate.

"How do you know?" I asked.

Emily turned back to me, the anger changing to sadness, tears in her eyes. "Kate and I were sisters, Noah. We talked. I know, okay?" She brought her hands to her eyes. "I don't want to talk about this now. I'll see you later."

She walked away quickly and disappeared into the church. Her reaction made me wonder if old Randall had suckered me into thinking he was a good guy when he wasn't.

"You think?" Carter asked, his gaze still on Randall.

"I don't know."

Randall glanced in our direction, raised his eyebrows in recognition, said something to the men he was standing with, and headed our way.

"But maybe I'll ask," I said.

Carter adjusted his sunglasses. "Oh, goodie."

Randall strode toward us, his eyes visibly red. "Noah, hello."

We shook hands. "Randall, this is my friend Carter Hamm. He was a friend of Kate's also."

They shook hands.

"I'm sorry about your wife," Carter said.

"Thank you," Randall said, his voice tight. "Thank you both for coming."

Carter and I nodded, that awkward bubble again forming around us. The sun felt hot on my neck, and I was sweating in my suit.

"Have you learned anything?" Randall asked quietly, his eyes darting from group to group.

"Not really," I lied. "This has all happened pretty quickly."

Randall nodded and smoothed his tie down his chest. "Sure. Please tell me if I can do anything to help."

Carter glanced at me, and I knew he was waiting for me to say something. I was having second thoughts because we were at a memorial service and I didn't want to take advantage of someone's vulnerability.

But Kate was dead and I was frustrated.

"Actually I do have a couple of questions."

He blinked several times, looking almost surprised that I'd taken him up on his offer, then shrugged. "Alright."

"The other night you said that Kate didn't want to be married anymore."

He nodded. "That's what she told me, yes."

"Any more thoughts on why she might've felt that way?"

"She didn't give me anything else," he said, rubbing his chin. "Never told me what she was unhappy about."

"Could it have been you?"

He blinked again and shoved a hand into his pocket. "I don't know, I guess."

I watched him. "Maybe something you'd done?"

Randall shifted his weight, his impatience starting to show. "Like?"

"What do you do in your spare time?" I asked.

"I don't follow."

"Water ski, collect art, knit," Carter said. "For example."

Randall glared at him. "Was I talking to you?"

"No. That was me talking to you. Pay attention."

Randall looked back to me. "Don't play with me, Noah. Not today. What do you wanna know?"

He'd raised his voice, and several looks were directed toward us.

"You and Kate had a good marriage?" I asked.

His jaw tightened. "I thought so."

"How good?"

The other hand disappeared into the other pocket. "I don't know how to answer that. I told you things were strained."

The sun was high in the sky and aimed directly at us.

"You cheat on her?" I asked.

Randall's cheeks flexed slightly, his jaw set. His eyes narrowed, and the sun wasn't the only thing that was hot.

"What the hell is this?" he growled.

"An investigation into your wife's death," I told him. "You asked if you could help."

Randall looked at Carter, who had settled into his imposing-but-nonchalant stance. I thought Randall wanted to hit Carter, but the more I thought about it, that didn't make sense because Randall didn't seem like a dumb guy.

Randall looked back at me. "Leave—now."

"You didn't answer my question," I said.

His right hand emerged from his pocket, his index finger pointing at me. "This is my wife's funeral. You wanna fuck around with me? Fine. But not here, not today."

"Then when?" I asked.

He jabbed the finger in my direction. "How about after I rip your fucking head off?" He spun on his heel and walked away from us.

I looked at Carter.

He adjusted his glasses. "How will you hear his answer if your head is detached?"

 *19*

Carter left the funeral before I did, mumbling something about having to be somewhere. I didn't ask where.

I hung around for a while, despite Randall's threat. I scanned the crowd looking for people who seemed out of place, who maybe didn't belong at Kate's funeral, who looked like a walking clue.

I went zero for three.

I was heading for my car when I heard someone call my name. I turned around and saw Emily coming toward me.

"Sorry," she said, as she reached me. "Didn't mean to yell."

"It's okay. What's up?"

She frowned, looking embarrassed. "I wanted to apologize for earlier."

"Earlier?"

She nodded. "Walking away from you and Carter like that. I just got too upset."

I watched the cars trickle out of the lot and down the hill. "I think you're allowed to be upset, Em."

"Well, thanks," she said, rubbing the back of her neck. "But I don't need to be rude, too."

"You weren't. It was fine."

The corners of her mouth flared into a small smile. "Always the nice guy. Even after living through my family."

"Even after." I paused for a moment. "At some point, I'd like to talk to you, though. About what you told me."

She turned and looked back at the church. "The thought of going back in there to help clean up isn't exactly enticing." She turned back to me. "How about now?"

"I didn't mean we had to do it right away, Emily. It can wait a day or two," I told her.

She waved a perfectly manicured hand in the air. "I'm fine. Really. I need to vent anyway. I'll buy you a drink at George's. Just let me grab my things."

She hurried back to the courtyard and quickly reemerged with a sweater and her purse. She reminded me of a more sophisticated Kate. They were both attractive, but Kate had always been the little sister, looking up to her sister with a sense of admiration and awe. Emily had always been more into the fashion trends and a little more into risk taking, a very cool older sister who didn't mind letting the little sister into her life.

I followed her BMW down the back side of Mount Soledad to the jammed up area at Prospect. La Jolla was a tiny strip on a cliff above the water, and traffic was ever present in the area. We parked up on Ivanhoe and walked back to the bluff-top restaurant at the northern edge of the La Jolla downtown district.

We walked out to the ocean terrace at George's, a rooftop bistro that drew raves for both its food and coastal scenery, small tables with candles dotting the deck. The restaurant faced north, up along La Jolla Shores all the way to where the cliffs at Torrey Pines jut out into the Pacific at Black's Beach. The sun looked tired, taking its time getting down in the west as we sat at a table near the railing.

"Pretty day for an ugly day," Emily said, sighing.

"Agreed."

The waitress appeared quickly and efficiently. Emily asked for a gin and tonic, and I requested a Jack and Coke. They were on the table in less than two minutes.

"So," Emily said, twirling the small straw in her drink. "Pretty weird, huh?"

I nodded. "Definitely."

She tossed the straw on the table, then sipped her drink. "I think I've gone through the emotional gamut. Sad, angry, irritated, confused, horrified, miserable. Did I miss anything?"

"Don't think so."

She shook her head, the sun reflecting off of the small pearls in her ears. "It just doesn't feel permanent."

I hadn't seen Kate in over ten years, but I felt the same way. "I know."

We sat there for a few minutes, nursing our drinks and watching the sun retreat behind the edge of the water. The breeze swept up off the ocean and felt cooler than normal. But maybe it was our mood.

"You didn't believe me about Randall, did you?" Emily said quietly, setting her drink on the glass top of the table.

I shrugged. "Not that I didn't believe you. I just didn't get that feeling from him when we met. What you said surprised me."

"He fools almost everyone," she said, the disdain in her voice unmistakable.

"Even Kate?"

She laughed softly, sadly. "Especially Kate." She finished her drink, pointed to it as our waitress walked by, and tried to smile. "The thing is, Kate was always the one you couldn't get anything past. I'm the ignorant one. But this time, someone fooled her."

I had never seen Emily as the ignorant one in the Crier family, but I knew firsthand how her parents could make you feel like something other than what you were.

"You said before that he was playing around from day one," I said. "Kate told you that?"

The waitress set two fresh drinks in front of us and scampered away.

"About six months in," Emily said, pulling at the napkin under the drink, "she started getting weird signals."

I sipped at the drink, the bourbon snaking a hot path into my stomach. "Like?"

"Paging him at the hospital and he took longer than usual to return the page," she said. "Some hang-ups at home when she answered the phone. He lost a shirt she had given him. Just very un-Randall-like things."

"What did she do?"

"Nothing at first," she said, her thin eyebrows arching slightly over her brown eyes. "She just blew it off as, I don't know, paranoia. But then she drove his car one Saturday. I don't remember what for. She found an earring in the passenger seat that wasn't hers."

The stupidity of spouses who cheat never fails to amaze me. You always get caught and it always ends badly. Always.

"She called me and told me that she'd found it," Emily said, still pulling at the napkin on the table. "I said to call him on it. It seemed pretty plain to me. I always liked Randall, but it just didn't sit right, you know?"

I nodded and sipped at my drink, the ice dancing off the inside of the glass.

She shaded her eyes from the bright explosion of the sunset. "So she did. And the asshole admitted it. No protests, no denials, no misdirection."

"What did Kate say?"

"She hardly said anything because he promised her

it wouldn't happen again," she said, the bitterness spiking in her words. "He swore it was just a one-time thing. And she bought it."

The Kate that I had known wasn't much for second chances with people. You were either honest with her or you weren't, and you didn't get a do-over if you weren't. But Randall had apparently qualified for a do-over.

"But it happened again," I said.

Emily nodded and emptied her drink. "Yep. Different girl, same story. Every time she caught him, he'd admit to it, then promise never again, then screw someone else."

"Why'd she stay with him?" I asked. "She knew he was messing around. That doesn't sound like Kate."

"It wasn't, Noah," she said, looking at me. "It wasn't like her at all. But she kept saying she thought this would be the time he'd turn around. She didn't want to get divorced."

"Because she loved him?"

The waitress slipped another drink in front of Emily, who seamlessly grabbed it and held it to her lips, soft wrinkles forming at the corners of her eyes as she frowned. "That and she didn't want to disappoint Mom and Dad. She enjoyed being the golden child."

The waitress had slid another drink in front of me as well. It was clear from Emily's tone that she viewed herself as the black sheep of the family. I had never gotten that impression when I'd been around the Criers a decade earlier, but I'd always been on the outside looking in. I wondered if she knew about Kate's heroin use, but decided against bringing it up at that moment. She'd just buried her sister, and no matter how she viewed her status in the family, shattering Kate's image might be too much for her to handle right now.

We watched the sun disappear completely, the ocean going from blue to black. All that was left of our view was the noise of the water kissing the base of the bluffs.

"I don't know, Noah," Emily said, shaking her head slowly. "I watched her get upset and angry. I became irate with her when she wouldn't do anything about it. But I couldn't make her leave him. There was something there and I never figured out what it was."

"So it was always different women?" I said, focusing on my words, making sure the bourbon stayed quiet.

"Until the end, yeah," she said, pushing her glass back and forth. "But the last few months, Kate gave me the impression that he might've developed a relationship with someone."

"The impression?"

Emily wiggled her hand in the air. "She wouldn't come out and say it directly. I think maybe it hurt too much. It was just the feeling that I had."

"Do you think she knew who it was?"

Emily paused, staring at her glass on the table for a moment. Then she said, "Yeah, I do."

We sat there, the breeze and fog surrounding us. I felt sorry for Kate, even though I wasn't sure why.

Maybe because I wasn't able to help her or because it sounded like she'd gotten herself into a situation that she didn't know how to get out of.

I had sympathy for Randall, too, but for him, I knew why. Because the next time I saw him, I was going to kick his ass.

 *20*

Emily asked me to drive her home because the gin had worked its magic on her. The bourbon had tried to do its thing with me, but I was gallantly fighting it off.

Her town house was in Del Mar, several miles up the coast from La Jolla. We took Torrey Pines Drive north, canopied by the giant trees, past the Scripps Institute and through the UCSD campus, and then fell onto Camino Del Mar, a thin strip of the old Pacific Coast Highway that let us glide right next to the moonlit water.

"When did you buy the town house?" I asked, guiding the Jeep over State Beach.

"Two years ago," she replied, shifting uncomfortably in the seat. "Nearly got married and then after we called it off, I dumped what little money I had into it."

"Why didn't the wedding happen?"

"We both chickened out two days before," she said, smiling ruefully. "It was the right thing to do. Neither of us wanted to be married. We were going through the motions more for show, I guess. Got caught up in the whole process and then didn't back out when we both knew we should've."

I changed lanes. "Your mom pissed?"

She laughed and tucked her blond hair behind her ear. "Mom came out of the womb pissed. I have only been able to add to it."

I remembered Kate having said something similar in high school, but I couldn't recall her exact words. There was always conversation about how her mom was regularly angry and unsatisfied.

Emily directed me off Camino Del Mar and up Carmel Valley Road to a cluster of stark white town houses perched at the top of a small hill just north of Torrey Pines State Beach. The homes were square and angular, something you might see above the Mediterranean.

"Come in for a second," Emily said. "There's something I want to show you."

I parked the car in the alley next to her garage. We took a narrow and steep set of stairs up to her door, which allowed me to notice that Emily possessed very nice legs.

I told the bourbon to shut up.

Her home was bright and modern. Blond wood served as the floor, an expensive-looking cream rug covering a portion of it in the middle of her living room. A black leather sofa rested against the one wall, affording a great view of the water to the west through floor-to-ceiling windows. A glass table centered the room, two tall bookshelves decorated with books and pictures resting on either side of the sofa.

"Another drink?" Emily asked, kicking off her shoes and heading toward the black-and-white kitchen that opened into the living room.

I knew that I shouldn't. I already felt awkward, a result of being at Emily's place and stealing glances at her legs.

"I think I've got some bourbon in here somewhere," she said, opening a cabinet.

Dammit. "Sure. That's fine."

I walked to the sliding door. A small terrace extended off the windows, two chairs and a table looking lonely on it.

"This is a great place," I said, watching the water roll under the moon.

"I bought it from a friend who moved to Boston," Emily responded, setting two glasses on the kitchen counter and filling them with ice. "She had to get rid of it quick. Only way I could've afforded it."

I walked over to look at the bookcases. Several pictures of Kate looked back at me. One was of her wedding day, Emily the maid of honor. Kate looked remarkable in a brilliant white gown with a matching smile. Randall stood next to her, tall, handsome, confident. It was the first picture of Kate that I'd seen in eleven years, and I couldn't rid myself of this tremendous sense of loss.

"Here," Emily said, coming up next to me and handing me a glass. She nodded at the picture. "Seems like a million years ago."

"I'll bet."

"She mentioned you that day."

I took a sip of the drink, the bourbon smoothing its way down my throat. "Her wedding day?"

Emily nodded. "Yeah. We were getting ready. I was helping her fasten her necklace and she said she wondered what you were doing."

It was an odd thing to hear, and I didn't know how to respond. I stared at the picture again.

"She should've called me," I said quietly.

"Noah," Emily said, putting a hand on my arm and reading my thoughts. "Do not for a second think any of this could be your fault."

I took another sip of the drink, thinking exactly that. "I don't."

She looked at me for a moment, her eyes at work, trying to discover if I was being truthful.

"I almost told her about that night when you came over," Emily said.

I shifted uncomfortably, guilt immediately seeping into my gut. "But you didn't?"

She shrugged. "I thought about it. Felt like I needed to come clean with her. But then I thought it was stupid, nothing really ended up happening, so I kept my mouth shut."

Standing in front of Kate's picture, I couldn't get myself to talk about it, as if she'd jump out of the photo and take a swing at me for nearly hooking up with her sister.

"You wanted to show me something," I reminded her, uncomfortable under her stare.

She paused for a moment, then nodded. "Yeah. Hang on."

She disappeared down the hallway. I took a deep breath, then finished my drink. I felt warm and fuzzy.

Emily reappeared, a small silver key in her hand. She held it out to me.

"What is it?" I asked.

"A key."

"Thanks. I mean a key to what?"

She shrugged. "I don't know. Kate spent the night here the first night she got into town because the hotel was full. I found it in the bedroom she slept in."

I laid it on the glass table and sat down on the sofa. "A stray key isn't a whole lot. Not unless you know where to stick it."

"I wish I could give it back to her," Emily said, rightfully ignoring my attempt at humor. "I know that's stupid but I just wish I could."

She leaned back into the sofa with me and we sat there quietly, each of us staring at the key on the table. I heard Emily's breathing start to chop up, then her hands went to her eyes, the tears spilling out over them. Her body shook, the sobs racking her and shaking the sofa.

I reached my arm around her and held her. She pressed against me and cried harder.

Finally, the tears stopped.

But neither of us moved.

I felt her head shift against my chest and against better judgment, I looked at her.

Her eyeliner had smudged at the corners of her eyes and her cheeks were flushed, bright red. Her blond hair was tossed over to one side.

We stared at one another, knowing what was coming, but not sure what to do about it.

Maybe not caring.

Maybe going back in time to finish something we had started a long time ago.

I don't know what the right thing to do would've been. I probably should've left. Or started talking, rambling on about anything. Ordering a pizza might not have been a bad idea.

But I didn't do any of those things.

Instead, we did other things.

 *21*

The night after Kate ended our relationship on Catalina, I'd gone to the Criers' house. I'm not sure what I planned on doing there. I wanted to see Kate, but I didn't know what I was going to say to her. Probably something petty and immature. But I knew I wanted to see her.

Only she wasn't there.

"Noah," Emily said, opening the door. "Didn't expect to see you."

Emily had intimidated me in high school. The older, sexier sister who could flirt effortlessly without meaning anything by it.

Or so I thought.

"Is Kate here?" I asked.

She opened the door wider. She was wearing a black bikini top and a bright yellow towel wrapped around her waist, exposing the taut muscles in her stomach.

She shook her head. "She's out with our parents. A few last-minute purchases before she leaves, I guess."

I felt my shoulders sag at the mention of Kate's leaving. "Oh."

"She told me about last night," Emily said. "I'm sorry."

I shoved my hands deep into my shorts pockets. "Yeah, me, too."

She pushed the door open wider. "You wanna come in? I was about to jump in the Jacuzzi. You can hang out till they get back."

I stood there feeling dumb, embarrassed. I knew I didn't have anything good to say to Kate. Whatever came out of my mouth was going to be either nasty or pathetic.

But I couldn't make myself leave.

"Okay," I said.

I followed her through the magnificent house that still felt unfamiliar to me, despite the countless hours I'd spent in it. We went downstairs to the enormous game room and out through the floor-to-ceiling sliders.

The Jacuzzi was at the far end of the pool, encircled by deep blue tiles and a concrete deck. The entire area provided a postcard view to the west, the Pacific Ocean seemingly at your fingertips and miles away at the same time.

Emily unwrapped her towel, dropped it on the deck, and slipped into the water, backlit by the lights embedded in the walls of the Jacuzzi. Her tan body looked like a shadow against the light blue of the bubbling water. She tilted her head back, submerging her long blond hair, then raised back up, pushing the hair away from her face toward the back of her head.

"You can come in if you want," she said, settling on the bench that ran the length of the inside of the tub.

I stepped out of my sandals and sat down on the ledge, dropping my legs into the warm water. "I'm good here."

She smiled. "So. You hate all of us now?"

I tried to laugh, but it came out as a snort. "No. I don't hate anybody."

"She didn't have to break up with you."

I shrugged. "Doesn't matter."

"I told her not to," she said, letting her hands rest on top of the water. "You don't deserve that, Noah. No one does."

I nodded, letting my eyes drop, unable to look at her. "Yeah."

"Of course, my parents are thrilled," she said, her tone getting sharper. "Little Kate does the right thing again."

I looked back up at her, shaking my head. "It doesn't matter."

She made a face and brought her hands together, a small wave of water splashing upward. "Gotta do what Mommy and Daddy say. Can't think for ourselves." She rolled her eyes. "Get chastised for that. Like me."

Kate never shared with me much about the family

dynamics in her home. I knew that Emily seemed more outgoing than Kate, but I had never seen it as anything more than that. Kate had never intimated that she felt like a favored child in her household, and I had always assumed that both girls were doted upon equally by both parents. Emily might've pushed the boundaries of her parents' patience more—breaking curfew or spending money a little more freely—but it was nothing that I figured earned more than a hard stare from her mother or father.

But Emily's tone suggested that maybe it was tougher than I knew to be the eldest Crier daughter.

"You were Kate's first mistake," she said.

I nodded, again looking away from her, again feeling the sting of the difference between my life and the Criers'.

Emily came across the water and touched my knee.

"I'm sorry," she said. "I didn't have to say that."

"It's alright," I mumbled.

"No, it's not," she said. "First my parents, then Kate. I don't need to be the last member of the family to treat you like shit."

I raised my eyes up and saw that she was closer than I expected, staring at me.

"It's okay, Emily," I said. "Really."

Her hand squeezed my knee slightly, and I felt the sudden shift in whatever it was that was going on between us. Emily may have been a concerned older sister, but she was acting differently toward me. And I may have been the forlorn rejected boyfriend, but I wasn't pushing her away.

"She's stupid, Noah," she said, moving closer so that I could feel her body against my leg. "She's blowing it."

The backyard was dark, save for the Jacuzzi lights illuminating us. The water lapped gently against the walls, and I was aware of how loud the stillness was.

"It's fine," I said, not looking away from her.

She shook her head slowly. "I'm not stupid."

She pushed harder against my leg under the water for a moment, then pushed herself out of the water onto the edge of the deck, next to me.

"Let me show you," she whispered, leaning into me.

Her mouth found mine, and I didn't resist. My stomach twisted with both guilt and excitement. She pulled me down into the water, lifted my shirt over my head. I distinctly remember seeing it float in the water next to us.

She moved back away from me, and I followed her to the other side of the Jacuzzi. When I reached her, the black bikini top was gone.

We kissed again, harder this time, some of my anger at Kate pushing me. Groping, grabbing, wet. Kate wouldn't have done this—she'd have been too worried about her parents finding us. Emily clearly didn't mind being half-naked with me.

A noise at the far side of the yard snapped in the air and startled me.

I pulled away from Emily. "What was that?"

She wrapped her arms tighter around my neck. "I don't know. I don't care." She twined her legs around mine, pushing hard against me. "Come on, Noah."

I knew I needed to leave, to jump out of that water, to walk out of the Crier house and never look back. I was angry at Kate for leaving me behind, for having a better opportunity than I had, for not having told me the truth. I knew having sex with her older sister wasn't going to solve my problems, alleviate my hurt. But I was also eighteen, pissed off at the world, and in a Jacuzzi with an attractive, willing girl.

Emily pressed her lips to my ear and whispered, "Come on."

I pulled away. "I gotta go."

She clung to me. "No you don't."

I untangled myself from her arms, water splashing around us, and pushed up onto the step and out of the Jacuzzi.

I turned around to her, water dripping off me onto the deck. "I'm sorry. I just can't."

My shirt was to her right in the water. She grabbed it, wadded it up, and flung it at me. "Figures. Whatever." Her mouth twisted sourly like she'd bit into something awful. "See you later."

I caught the wet shirt but didn't put it on. I turned and walked back through the house, out the front door, and down to my car.

I don't know why I left that night. I was furious at Kate, at her parents, and Emily was a willing participant. But something about it didn't feel right. Maybe it was the fear of being caught. Maybe I just couldn't get over how I felt about Kate.

But walking away from Emily felt like the right thing to do that night.

Eleven years later, though, staying with Emily felt like the only thing to do.

 *22*

I woke to a note on Emily's pillow.

I'LL CALL YOU. E.

If I'd been the first to wake, I would've left the same note, just with an "N."

I was alone in her house, and it just didn't fit. I wasn't sure that the previous hours had felt right— except of course for the physical part, which always did—and I needed to breathe.

I dressed quickly, grabbed the key she'd given me off the coffee table, and dashed out the front door. I knew I probably looked silly jogging to my car, but I didn't want to run into Emily coming back from wherever she'd gone. I wasn't prepared for that meeting yet.

PCH was empty at eight in the morning, and I made it back to Mission Beach in half an hour. I slipped into my shorts, grabbed the six-foot squash tail from beside the sofa, and walked down to the water, letting the salt and waves fill my senses as I waded in.

I dropped onto my board and paddled out. I ducked under the small waves that were rolling in, letting the icy shock of the Pacific ride up my spine and into my ears with a roar. The chill of the early morning air hit me as I emerged from the waves, making my body tingle.

I saw Carter pop up on the horizon just to my right, sliding down the face of a slow four footer that was breaking south toward the jetty. It closed out on both sides of him and he dropped off the board into the water, slapping the surface with his giant palm, frustrated. He saw me maneuvering in his direction and waited for me to reach him.

"Dude," he said, wiping the water from his face and jumping back on his board. "Where you been?"

"You're out early," I said, avoiding the question.

"Break looked good."

"Is it?"

"No. Only been out for twenty minutes or so, but the sets are slow and choppy. Getting tired of waiting for it to get better."

We floated for a moment, the water swelling gently beneath us, and I knew we were both waiting for an answer to his question.

"Emily's," I said finally.

He raised a wet eyebrow. "All night?"

"All night."

He ran a massive hand through his soaked yellow hair, the water running out of it like it was coming off a Lab's back. "That's interesting."

"She gave me a key."

"Jesus. You must rock in the sack."

"I do, but it's not a key to her place. It's a key that Kate left behind."

I nodded toward the horizon. We paddled out beyond the break and spun ourselves around so that we were facing the shore again, hoping that a decent set would roll in behind us.

"What's it unlock?" he asked.

"Don't know."

"Well, good thing you have it then."

"I know."

We paddled forward a little, trying to find the right spot in the lineup.

"How did this occur, Lover Boy?"

I shrugged. "Not sure. We had a few drinks, went back to her place to get the key, I saw pictures of Kate on her wedding day, she cried a little, and then, shazam."

"Shazam?"

"Shazam."

Two small swells rolled under us, barely rising above the surface of the ocean. Not even close to something I'd consider paddling in front of.

"Was this a grief thing for you guys? Or just picking up where you left off in her Jacuzzi way back when?"

I spun sideways so I was parallel to the beach, eyeing both the shoreline and the open water. "I don't know. Probably both of those, I guess."

"What'd she say about it?"

"I woke up solo and got the hell out of there."

He almost grinned. "Sounds like she was as weirded out about it as you are."

I looked at him. "You think I'm weirded out?"

He glanced back behind him at the waves, ignoring my question. "Finally. Here we go."

He was inside, so the first was his. He started paddling, his huge arms propelling him through the water, as the wave picked him up and carried him away.

I shifted so I was facing the beach again and moved my arms easily through the water. I felt the wall of water sweep in behind me and lift me up. I popped up on the board and my stomach dropped with excitement as I skimmed down the face of the wave, my back to the beach as I moved down the fall line at the bottom of the wave. I shifted my weight and used my right foot to snap the board back into the wave and through the lip at the top, the white water and salt spraying my face. I came back down and zigzagged for another ten feet or so before the wave died and disappeared.

I dropped to my stomach and swiveled around, heading back out to the break. I felt Carter paddle up on my right.

"Yeah, I think you're weirded out about it," he said.

I was, and I knew I wouldn't be able to hide it. I had spent the night with the older sister of my dead ex-girlfriend, whose murder I was supposed to be investigating. I was very close to becoming Jerry Springer material.

We paddled back out, side by side.

"How does this change your assignment?" Carter said.

"I don't know that it does."

"Just asking."

Other than making things awkward between Emily and myself, I didn't think it would affect looking into Kate's death. Emily and I both wanted the same thing with that.

It was what Emily and I wanted with each other that I wasn't sure of.

 **23**

"Let me see the key."

An hour later, we were in my living room, both in dry clothes, and Carter was sitting on the couch.

I grabbed the key off the counter and tossed it to him.

He held it in his palm and flipped it over a couple of times. "You sure it doesn't belong to Emily's heart?"

"You sure you don't want me to kick you in the ear?"

He snorted. "She knows it was Kate's?"

"No. She knows Kate left it at her place before she went to the hotel."

"Can I hang on to it? I know a guy who might be able to get you something on it."

I looked at him. "You know an expert on keys?"

"Something like that."

I shook my head, surprised that I was surprised. "Yeah. Have at it."

He closed it in his palm and nodded in the direction of the kitchen. "Message on the machine for you."

"Did you listen to it?"

"Of course. I had to come in and get something to eat before I hit the water. I saw the blinking light and couldn't resist."

"Then tell me what the message is."

He made a face. "But then I'd feel like your secretary or something."

"You need to do something to earn your keep."

"I don't live here."

"Fooled me."

He pointed at the machine. "It's that cop you used to sleep with."

Or, as her colleagues called her, Detective Santangelo.

"What did she say?" I asked.

"Wants you to call her."

I looked at the phone, hoping it didn't work. "Right away?"

"As always."

I went over and picked up the phone, frowned when I got a dial tone. I hit the machine, listened to Liz's very serious voice, and dialed the number she'd left.

She answered on the first ring. "Santangelo."

"Braddock," I fired back.

She paused for a moment, maybe trying to figure out who it was or maybe not finding me funny. Hard to tell.

"I need you to come in," she said.

"From out of the rain?"

She sighed heavily. "Noah. I'm not screwing around. Will you come down?"

"Depends. What happens if I don't?"

"Then I'll send someone with cuffs to get you."

The neighbors had probably grown weary of seeing me with the police, and I didn't want to rattle them so early in the morning.

"I'll come."

"Carter with you?" she asked.

"Yeah."

"Bring him, too."

"I'm not his chaperone," I told her.

"No, you're more like his mother. Bring him." She hung up.

"Detective Santangelo wishes to see us," I told Carter, grabbing my car keys off the table.

He stood up and stretched like a cat, his hands nearly touching the ceiling. "What if I don't wish to be seen?"

"She didn't give me that option," I said, heading for the door.

He groaned. "Well, that's not fair."

"Come on. You can tell her to her face."

He grinned. "Ah. A challenge."

 *24*

San Diego Police headquarters is located in the heart of downtown on Broadway, a couple blocks from the courts and jail and right near the Michael Graves–designed Horton Plaza. San Diegans liked to point out the strange shopping mall as a defining image of the city, but I could never get past the fact that the biggest obstacle in building the structure had been figuring out where to move the homeless folks so they wouldn't be hovering around a major tourist attraction.

Square, bland, and unimaginative, headquarters could not look any more governmental. Liz's office occupied a spot at the end of the hall on the third floor. Her head was down, staring at some paperwork on her desk.

"We're looking for the Pirates of the Caribbean," I said. "Can you point us in the right direction?"

She glanced up, pulling her dark hair away from

her face and over her shoulder. "Shut the door behind you."

Her office was small. A perfect square, with cheap cabinets in each of the four corners, her metal desk in the middle so that she could see anyone coming in. No pictures on the walls, only a city-issued calendar, with pictures of the zoo.

Carter and I sat in the two chairs facing her desk. Her chair looked considerably more comfortable.

"You need to back off," she said, her eyes on me.

I scooted my chair back a couple of inches. "That good enough?"

Her mouth screwed into a tight circle, a clear sign that whatever patience she had allotted for me was now gone. Same old, same old.

She unscrewed her mouth. "Noah, Costilla is off-limits to you."

"Officially?"

"Officially, unofficially, on the record, off the record," she said. "Any way you want it. You go near him again, you're done."

She looked at Carter. "And before you open that sinkhole you call a mouth, that means you, too."

Carter stared back at her with no expression.

"Why?" I asked.

"Because."

"Gee, Mommy, I need something better than that," I said.

She leaned forward on the desk, the silver bracelets on her wrists jingling softly. "Because I've got an ID on you both in San Ysidro and I'll arrest you if you so much as wink at him."

"Bullshit," Carter said. "You got an ID, you'd arrest us now."

"Contrary to the opinion of the rest of this city, I'm not looking to lock you up," she said. "As far as I'm concerned, one of Costilla's guys biting it isn't such a bad thing. But I can sit you both in a cell if I need to. Those pain-in-the-ass twins you call friends, too, if I want."

"So if I say no," I said, "then you're going to arrest us right now."

She nodded.

I looked at Carter. He shrugged.

I looked back at Liz. "No."

We all sat there. No one came rushing in with handcuffs and jumpsuits. I turned around to make sure. Nobody came in. They wouldn't have fit in the room anyway.

Liz shifted uncomfortably in her comfortable chair and leaned back into it again. "He's Federal, Noah."

"So?"

"He's Federal with our cooperation. Specifically, my cooperation."

"So?"

She slapped her hand on the desk. "Goddammit, Noah. Don't fuck around with me on this. He is off-limits. The Feds are on him, I am assisting, and they don't want to see you near him. So keep your fucking ass far, far away from him."

Carter looked at me. "Couldn't she have left this on the machine?"

I ignored him, because I knew Liz was serious. The flames coming out her ears were my first clue.

"Okay," I said to her. "Off-limits."

She watched me, suspicion shooting out her eyes.

With good reason.

"But only if you answer me one thing," I said.

Her mouth twitched. "What?"

"Were the Feds looking at Kate, too?"

She blinked once, shifted her neck like there was a kink in it. "You won't get within a hundred miles of him?"

"Two hundred."

She paused, staring at me like she was trying to decide if I was telling her the truth. "Kate was working for them."

"The FBI?" I asked.

She let out a deep breath. "No. It's DEA."

If she had jumped over the desk and kissed Carter, it would've surprised me less. "No way."

"She was inside."

"Then how did she die?" Carter asked.

She set her elbow on the desk, made a fist, and leaned her chin on it, her face drawn. "They screwed up."

Her words hung in the air like a neon sign. I knew by the way that she said it, that whoever had screwed up, whoever had let Kate die, wouldn't admit to it. Collateral damage in a bigger operation.

I felt my chest tighten. "Back up. What the hell was she doing inside?"

"I can't tell you."

"The fuck you can't," I said, louder than I'd intended.

Her eyes widened, and she lifted her head off of her chin. "Beg your pardon?"

"You drop that cannonball on me and then tell me you can't explain?" I said. "Like I'm just supposed to accept it, not be surprised by it? You give me more, or any promise I made to you is off the table."

Liz shrugged. "Then I'll arrest you both." She looked at Carter. "Are you really dumb enough to think that someone wouldn't notice that shitpiece you drive?" She turned back to me. "You don't believe me? Try me."

I wanted to reach across the desk and grab her by the throat. Maybe throw something at the wall behind her, something to let her know how badly she was pissing me off.

But none of that would get me closer to the reason for Kate's death.

"So, you'll tell me that she got killed because someone screwed up somewhere, but you won't tell me anything about what she was doing?" I asked quietly. "Not even off the record?"

She shook her head slowly. "I can't, Noah."

"Then you know I won't leave it alone."

She thought about that, then nodded.

"And if you catch me near Costilla, you'll toss on the cuffs," I said.

She nodded again.

I stood up, and Carter did the same.

"Then catch me if you can," I said and we left.

 **25**

"Married to an asshole, a drug user, and working for the G-men. Not exactly the old Kate," Carter said.

"No, not exactly," I mumbled back to him.

We were headed north on the 5, Sea World and Mission Bay on the west side, beckoning the tourists that flocked to America's Finest City. Traffic was moving smoothly for once but it didn't improve my mood. Nothing was making sense, and I was getting angrier with each new revelation. I felt like the more I discovered about Kate, the further I got from the truth.

"Would they really use someone like Kate inside a world like Costilla's?" I asked, unable to shake the question from my brain.

Carter shifted in his seat and tugged at the seat belt. "They'd use whoever they could to get what they need. Male, female, young, old. Doesn't matter to them."

I nodded absently.

"The ME said Kate was using drugs, right? DEA was using her for something in connection with Costilla. That says to me she got caught in something," Carter said. "An immunity deal maybe?"

I thought about that for a moment. "Maybe. Just seems odd. What did they catch her with that would justify putting her under the gun like that?"

"It had to have been some heavy shit," Carter said. "But I can't imagine why the law enforcement geniuses would think she'd make a great undercover candidate. All of a sudden, some upper-crust white woman shows up and tries to secretly fit in? Fucking brilliant."

The wind from the open windows whipped through my hair as I turned everything over in my mind. If Kate was involved in drugs and got caught, it would make sense that there might be some sort of a deal made. But I thought a court testimonial would make a lot more sense than sending her into the lion's den.

"Yeah. Why would you put someone like her in a position like that?" I said. "How the hell would she know what she was doing?"

"If a deal was set up," Carter said, "someone would've needed to do some string pulling."

I was getting around to that thought. "Like Daddy Crier."

We drove in silence for a moment, cutting under the twisting curl of concrete that jutted off the freeway and up to the bluffs of La Jolla.

"You think Costilla found out what Kate was doing?" I asked.

"Maybe," Carter said.

"But . . ."

"But don't you think he would've left a message?"

"Like?"

Carter waved a hand in the air. "A message that said 'I know who she was and what she was doing.' She was in a trunk, strangled. That's not exactly a Colombian necktie."

I considered that. No murder was mundane or ordinary, but Carter had a point. Now that we knew that the twists in Kate's life were more severe, the way she had died, the way I'd found her, didn't seem that dramatic.

"Not to change the subject or anything," Carter said, interrupting my thoughts. "But that Cadillac has been with us for a while, dude." He reached under his seat and retrieved my gun, a 9mm Glock 17, setting it in his lap.

I glanced in the rearview mirror. A white Cadillac was two cars back, in our lane. "How long?"

"Long enough to be a problem." He opened the glove box and pulled his gun out. He held the .45 HK Mark 23 low against the door.

I moved over into the fast lane. The Cadillac sped up and moved into our blind spot, trying to hide.

I was trying to figure out what to do when the blue van in front of us hit its brakes.

Jamming my foot on the brakes, I turned the wheel

to the left, sliding onto the shoulder and next to the median. The van moved left in the same direction, anticipating where I'd go, blocking us in the front. The rear doors opened slightly and two gun barrels emerged in the tight space.

The Cadillac cut over and screeched to a halt diagonally behind us.

Trapped.

Carter tossed my gun at me. I rolled out of the door, staying close to the car and the ground. The windshield of my Jeep shattered in seconds, the bullets flying like irritated hornets from both directions, the shards of glass spilling into the front seat.

Carter followed me out the driver's-side door, a small streak of blood making its way down his neck. We had about three feet to maneuver in between my car and the concrete median.

I rose up quickly into the open window of the door and fired into the van. Carter swiveled and fired into the Cadillac behind us. I ducked down, and we both stayed close to the car, bullets flying over us.

"We gotta move," I said. "We're fish in a bowl right here."

More bullets crackled against the pavement behind my car, and we both flinched. Carter looked at the median.

"I'll cover," he said. "You get over this and move backward toward the Cadillac. Come at them from behind."

I nodded. He rose up and started firing, first at the van, then the Cadillac. I took one short step and flung myself over the median, praying that I wouldn't spill out into the southbound fast lane.

Cars were stopping on both sides of the freeway, watching our little ambush. I heard metal on metal from a distance and knew someone had been following too closely. Voices were yelling but they sounded far away and unintelligible.

I crab-crawled about fifty feet on the pavement, my eyes on the top of the median. I spun when I knew I was well past the Cadillac and rose up over the edge.

Two teenagers, clad in white T-shirts, baggy chinos, and blue bandanas around their heads, were behind the open doors of the Cadillac, automatic weapons pointed in Carter's direction. I took a deep breath and squeezed the trigger. The one on the driver's side dropped to the ground, clutching his leg. His partner looked in my direction from the other side of the car.

I saw Carter's head come up briefly, then go down when more shots from the van were gunned in his direction. I fired through the Cadillac at the passenger. He returned the fire, then sidestepped toward the van, staying low on the passenger side of the Cadillac, then my Jeep. A few more shots flew from the back windows of the van, the rear doors opened more, and the shooter from the Cadillac dove in. The doors shut and the van screeched away, whizzing between the stopped cars on our side of the freeway, smoke flowing from the tires. They maneuvered to the far right lane, gunned the engine again, and sped north.

All lanes of traffic on both sides of the freeway were blocked now, cars pointed in every possible direction, people's eyes wild with fear. The air was heavy with the smell of burnt rubber and cordite. Sweat was pouring down my back. I hopped the median and kicked the gun away from the kid I'd shot as he writhed in pain, his thigh leaking blood rapidly. I looked at his face but didn't recognize him.

"Carter, it's clear," I yelled.

I expected some wiseass line about taking so long or my driving getting us into this.

But the only response I got was the sound of sirens in the distance.

26

Four bullets had hit Carter, two in the chest and two in the stomach. I blanched at the red puddle spilling out from beneath his body on the concrete of the freeway, his skin already a light gray as his system went into shock. He mumbled incoherently for a minute as I pressed on the bloody holes in his chest, before he shut his eyes and passed out.

Police and ambulances arrived in bunches. Traffic was rerouted. People were yelling and screaming. A helicopter grew larger above us, finally landing on the southbound side of the highway. The paramedics loaded Carter onto a backboard, passed him over the median to another set of paramedics. I followed them into the helicopter before anyone could suggest otherwise.

LifeFlight flew us to the UCSD Trauma Unit, a team of technicians working feverishly over his body in the cramped aircraft. I grabbed a towel off the floor of the helicopter and wiped the blood off my hands. Then I grabbed a handle suspended from the roof and tried not to throw up.

After I'd waited an hour outside the surgical unit, a doctor emerged and told me that Carter was a mess. Lots of internal damage, lots of bleeding. They were going to watch him in the critical care unit and see what happened.

I sat in a waiting room and tried to quell the nausea in my gut. I kept glancing at the dried blood under my fingernails, trying not to think about who it belonged to or why it was there. There is a certain uselessness that accompanies sitting quietly in a waiting area, and I was settling into it awkwardly when Liz got off the elevator.

She wore a dark green sweater and black jeans, black framed glasses on her face. I used to accuse her of wearing them to appear smarter, but they did look good on her.

A thick, short black man dressed in tan slacks, a white T-shirt, and a navy blazer trailed her. A T-shirt that read I'M A COP! would've been less conspicuous.

"Noah," Liz said, sitting down across from me. "How is he?"

"Not good."

She gestured at her guest. "This is my partner, Detective John Wellton. He's working Kate's case with me."

We shook hands. Cool blue eyes stared out at me from skin the color of a Hershey bar, the contrast startling.

The fact that he couldn't have been over five feet tall didn't help.

"Good to meet you," he said, not meaning it, his expression dour. "Sorry about your friend."

He stood up straight and puffed out his chest. Almost made up for the fact that his feet wouldn't touch the ground if he sat on the chair next to Liz.

"He still in surgery?" Liz asked.

I shook my head. "Came out about an hour ago. They need him to stabilize before they can do more. He's in the CCU."

She thought about it. "He's tough. He'll make it."

"I know," I said, hoping she was right.

"Mr. Braddock," Wellton said, pulling a notebook from his pocket. "Did you get plates on the van that left the scene?"

"No, it happened too fast."

He nodded, scribbling quickly. "How about the assailants? Recognize them?"

"No," I said, glancing at Liz. "Looked like gangbangers, though. Teenagers. They were in the Cadillac. I couldn't see the faces of the guys from the van."

"Probably Costilla," Liz said, leaning forward. "He's used them as his little soldiers before. Cheap and nasty."

I nodded absently. A gurney emerged from the elevator, surrounded by people shouting at one another. They disappeared quickly through the swinging doors.

"Can you give me descriptions?" Wellton asked, peering over the notepad at me.

I shrugged. "Teen, male, Hispanic. That's about it."

He looked at me, the chest puffing out again, annoyed. "That's it?"

I glared at him, not wanting to relive the afternoon. "Take the kid I hit. Draw a picture. Make three copies. That's what I saw."

"How'd your buddy get hit?" he asked, scribbling again.

I looked at Liz. "Some bullets flew into him."

Liz covered her mouth with her hand and avoided my eyes.

Wellton took a step in my direction. "Hey, wiseass, you left a crime scene to ride with your friend. Nobody hassled you about that. But now you owe us. I need some information from you. You can either talk to me here or I can take you downtown."

I stood up. "You and what step stool?"

The notepad slipped from his hand to the floor and he put a finger in my gut. Probably aiming for my chest. I slapped it away.

Liz jumped up. "Alright, knock it off." She looked at Wellton. "Give us a minute, John?"

He stared up at me, holding his ground. If I'd had a drink, I would've set it on his head. He took a step back, picked up his notepad, and walked down the hallway.

I pointed in his direction. "I will kick Gary Coleman's ass if I get peppered with any more questions tonight."

"He's wired a little tight," Liz admitted. "He's a good guy, though. He can help."

I sat back down in the chair. "Whatever."

She sat across from me. "Definitely gangbangers?"

I took a deep breath. "Looked like it."

"What kind of guns?"

I pictured the ambush. "Automatics. Hung over the shoulder. They were just spraying. They weren't good shooters."

She nodded. "Sounds right."

"You have the one I shot?"

"Yeah, but he's in surgery," she said. "You gave him a permanent limp. We have to wait."

We sat there in silence for a few minutes, looking at everything but one another. I never would've said it, but her company helped.

"They lost her," she said finally.

I looked at her. "What?"

"Kate was in the car with two of Costilla's men in Tijuana," she said, her eyes staring me down from behind the glasses. "Since they were on the Mexican side of the border, DEA took the coverage. We had her on the U.S. side."

She shifted in her seat and folded her hands in her lap. "Costilla's men must've nailed the tail. They shook them off somewhere in the downtown area and she was gone for three days." She paused. "Until you found her. We were searching in Mexico when she was right here under our noses."

I let that sink in. It hurt.

"Why was she there, Liz?" I asked.

She stood up. "I gave you all I'm giving you."

I thought about it and nodded slowly. She'd said more than she'd needed to, especially when I had been a jerk in her office earlier. "Okay. Thanks."

"We had to tow your car down to impound for investigation. I can have someone take you to a rental agency," she said. "Come down to the station tomorrow. We'll do the report then, alright?"

"Yeah." I watched her walk toward the elevator. "Liz?"

She turned back to me. "What?"

"Thanks for coming," I told her. "Carter would appreciate it."

A tired smile formed on her lips. "No, he wouldn't. But thanks for saying it anyway."

She disappeared into the elevator.

 **27**

I left my cell number with the hospital staff and asked them to call me if anything changed with Carter. I fought the guilt of leaving the hospital and let one of Liz's officers drive me over to an Avis counter at the Embassy Suites on La Jolla Village Drive.

After fifteen minutes of paperwork and avoiding the various sales pitches of the rental agent, I walked out to the lot with keys to a Chevy Blazer. It had tinted windows and gray leather interior that still smelled new. I missed the aroma of salt and wax in the Jeep as I pointed the SUV in the direction of the Crier home.

When Kate and I had dated, I had dreaded going to her house. The size of it, the smell of the money, the disapproving looks all had made me uncomfortable. I didn't have the nerve to stand up to it when I was a teenager, the guts to tell them I was good enough for their youngest daughter. Now, getting out of the Blazer, I knew that nothing in that house would prevent me from saying what I wanted to say.

Ken answered the door, barefoot and wearing navy shorts and a tan Polo shirt. "Noah."

"We need to talk."

He waved me in, and we went to the large living room across from the entryway. Two white-leather sofas faced one another, divided by a marble-topped coffee table. Several large abstract paintings hung on the wall, reds and yellows tied together in ugly formation. The color on the canvasses couldn't remove the sterile feel of the room.

Ken sat down across from me on one of the sofas. "What can I do for you?"

"Why was Kate here in San Diego?" I asked.

He shrugged. "I'm not exactly sure. We assumed it was to spend the week with us." He paused for a moment. "She probably needed some time away from Randall as well."

"How did you get her out of it?" I asked.

He frowned, half circles at the corners of his eyes. "I'm sorry?"

"How did you get her out of whatever trouble she was in?"

"I'm confused."

"No, you're not," I said. "Kate had some sort of deal working with the DEA. The way I figure, she got caught in something bad. Why else would she have been working for them?"

He thought about that and decided to lie. "Noah, I have no idea—"

I stood up. "I quit." I started walking toward the door.

"Noah," he said, his voice harsher. "Hold on."

I turned around. "Tell me the truth, now, Ken. Right now. Marilyn didn't tell me everything. I've learned more from staying away from you two than talking to you. I know Kate was involved in something that was way over her head. And I have a pretty good feeling you're the only one that could've set it up. You wanna screw around with me, then I'm done helping you."

He leaned back in the sofa, the leather collapsing around his body. "She was arrested six months ago."

I walked back into the room and sat across from him.

"Heroin," he said, his mouth tightening. "She got stopped for speeding up in Marin County. It was under the front passenger seat and was visible when the cop came to the window for her license and registration. There was enough to charge her with intent to sell. A felony."

I felt my eyes twitch. The idea that Kate had had that much heroin didn't seem real to me.

Ken turned and stared out the massive window. The view looked down over the west end of Mount Soledad and La Jolla Shores, barely glimpsing the far edge of the Pacific.

He shook his head. "I couldn't let her go to jail."

"What was she doing with the drugs, Ken?" I asked. "Did she have a problem?"

He laughed bitterly. "Oh, she had a problem. From what I learned, she experimented with it during college. Battled with it from then on."

"She couldn't shake it?" I asked, trying to picture a strung-out Kate in an Ivy League dorm room.

"She tried rehab several times, but never lasted more than six months clean." He looked at me. "It was killing her. Until about a year ago."

I didn't understand. "What happened?"

He smiled sadly. "She kicked it, on her own. No help from me or doctors or counselors. Just dug in her heels and stopped."

That sounded more like the Kate I had known.

"Then what was she doing with heroin in her car?" I asked.

His mouth puckered for a moment, like he was trying to get down some awful food. "It wasn't hers."

I looked at him, doubtful. "From what you've just told me, that's pretty hard to buy into."

"I know. But it wasn't hers, Noah," he said, his voice tight.

"Whose was it, then?"

He turned to the window again, shaking his head as if he still couldn't believe what he was about to say. "It was Randall's."

I leaned back into the sofa and listened.

"Randall had a . . . problem, as well," Ken said. "When they first got married, they were perfect for one another. Just a couple of yuppie junkies with too much money."

He licked his lips, as if he were trying to get the taste out of his mouth. "I'd really given up. Figured she was going to die, thought we'd get a call in the middle of the night and have to pull her out of the gutter. I tried to do what I could. But it didn't matter." He paused. "When Kate cleaned up, I assumed Randall had, too."

"But he hadn't," I said.

"I'm not exactly sure," he said. "Kate said he had, but I think he may have been dabbling, if that's the appropriate term."

"Why?"

He shrugged. "Just his appearance when we went to visit. One day he looked fine, next he looked like crap. I learned to recognize the signs after dealing with Kate."

He rubbed his hand over his face. When I was in high school, I had alternately wanted to impress Ken Crier and kick his ass. Now I just felt sorry for him.

"Anyway, it was his car Kate was driving. She told me she didn't know it was there and she was just as surprised to see it under the seat as the cop was. We were at a point where I knew she wasn't lying to me anymore."

"But the police didn't believe her?"

His eyes fired up again. "She covered for his ass, Noah. She took the blame."

"Why?"

"Because he was on probation," he said, almost spitting it out. "*Is* on probation. Got arrested about a year and a half ago for possession, pleaded down to a lesser charge."

I tried to take it all in. Kate and Randall were both users. Maybe dealers. The good doctor had gotten caught and escaped with a tiny slap—as long as it didn't happen again.

"So she covered for him," I said.

"Yeah."

"And he let her."

An ugly smile twisted his mouth. "And he let her."

Cheating on Kate and then getting her into this crap. I now had two reasons to beat the crap out of Randall Tower.

"I set it up," Ken said. "I got the San Diego DA to arrange with the DA in Marin. They brought her down. She had to make four buys."

"They miked her and everything?"

"The whole deal."

I could feel the anger building in my stomach. She'd finally gotten her life together and ended up dying, trying to cover her husband's ass.

"And Randall let her," I said again.

Ken Crier nodded slowly, not saying anything, a mixture of anger, guilt, and sadness playing across his features.

We sat there for a moment, him staring out at nothing, me trying to remember the girl I'd loved in high school.

"What was going to happen after the last buy?" I asked.

He swung his gaze back to mine, his eyes red. "They were going to take the recorded conversations and the drugs she bought and hopefully get Costilla. They thought this was their chance to take him down."

"Was she going to testify?"

"Not in court. It was going to be done through paperwork and by video. She wouldn't have to enter the courtroom. Once they had what they needed, she was done and clear. She told me she was going to leave Randall, to start all over . . ." His voice trailed off.

"What?" I asked.

His eyes were someplace else, maybe back to that last conversation with his youngest daughter. "I thought maybe she was going to try to find you, Noah."

 *28*

I walked out of the Criers' home before it swallowed me whole.

I headed home, stopping at the deli on Law to buy a twelve pack of Red Trolley. I wasn't sure that twelve was all I'd need to wash the day out of my head, but I figured it would be a good start.

When I walked into my place, the first thing I noticed was that the screen door to the patio stood halfway open.

Silently, I set the beer on the floor and pulled my gun from the small of my back. I checked the bedroom and bathroom and found nothing. I moved slowly toward the patio and peeked out the door.

Emily was sitting on one of the lounge chairs.

"Emily?"

She turned in my direction and stood up. "Noah." She looked at the gun. "Did I do something wrong?"

I ducked back in the house, replaced the safety,

and set it on the dining room table, then joined Emily outside.

"No, sorry," I said. "Just being careful."

She studied me for a second. "What's wrong?"

I shook my head. "Nothing."

A braid of long blond hair hung over her shoulder. She wore a red T-shirt and white walking shorts. White leather sandals matched the shorts. She stuck her hands in her pockets. "Should I not be here?"

A good question that I was having trouble finding the answer to.

"It's fine," I told her. I pointed to the chair she'd been sitting in when I'd arrived. "I'm sorry. Sit."

She did, not taking her eyes off me.

"Carter's in the hospital," I said, sitting in the chair next to her.

Her mouth tightened. "What happened?"

I told her.

When I was through, she asked, "Is this because of Kate?"

"I think so."

She leaned back into her chair, shaking her head. "I can't believe it. I'm so sorry."

I nodded, as I pulled my phone out of my pocket and set it on the small resin table. I stared at it for a moment, wondering what I would hear when it eventually rang.

"Can I do anything?" Emily asked.

"No. The hospital will call when they have something to tell me. Just have to wait." I stared out at the horizon, the sun a faint yellow smudge hovering over the water.

She reached over and touched my arm. "He'll be okay."

I tried to smile. "Probably." I changed the subject. "What's up? Why are you here?"

A reluctant smile emerged. "No reason, really. Just thought I'd come see you. I mean, after last night and everything."

Last night seemed like last year.

"Uh, yeah," I mumbled, at a loss for what to say.

She tugged gently on her braid. "Weird, huh?"

"That's one word for it."

"But good," she said, her eyes searching my face.

"But good."

We watched the smudge disappear completely, tucking in behind the blue of the water.

"So now what?" I asked, breaking the silence.

"I'm not sure," Emily said. "I was thinking we could talk about it, but now, with Carter . . . it doesn't seem like the best time."

I agreed, never being one for those kinds of discussions even when my best friend wasn't in the hospital. "No, it doesn't."

"You want me to leave?"

I shifted in the chair. "Em, I'm not sure about this whole you-and-me thing yet. There's so much going on right now that I need to go slow."

"I didn't mean should I stay so we can sleep together again," she said, staring at me. "I'm all for the slow thing, too." She paused for a moment and glanced toward the water. "All I could think about today was Kate. I felt like . . . I don't know. Every time I thought of you today, about last night, I felt guilty." She looked back at me. "So all I meant was that I wondered if maybe you wanted to be by yourself."

My assumption made me feel silly, and I felt better that we were thinking along the same lines. I stood up, walked inside, grabbed the carton of beer, and brought it out to the patio with a bottle opener. I opened two and handed her one.

"Company would be good," I said. "Stay for a while."

So she did.

 **29**

Emily left around midnight, and my cell phone rang at six the next morning.

I fumbled around on the nightstand but couldn't find it. I sat up and realized it wasn't in the room. I found the phone on the dining room table next to my gun.

"Hello?"

"Mr. Braddock?"

"Yeah, who's this?"

"This is Beth from UCSD Trauma. The chart said to call this number if there was any status change with Patient Hamm."

My stomach tightened. "Right. How is he?"

"He's awake."

"I'll be there in half an hour."

I skipped my morning session on the lonely water and made the drive to UCSD in twenty-five minutes. Beth directed me to Carter's room and told me I only had fifteen minutes to talk with him.

His head rolled in my direction when I entered. He was stretched out on an uncomfortable-looking bed, a pale blue blanket pulled up to his waist. A tube snaked its way into his bare chest, an IV line making its way into each of his arms. His skin was pale, his eyes bloodshot. An oxygen tube curled into his nostrils.

He tried to smile anyway. "Dude."

I pulled a chair from under the window over next to the bed. "Dude yourself."

His eyes did a slow take around the room and then landed back on me. "This sucks."

"I'll say."

He swallowed hard. "Doctor said I'm going back to surgery this morning."

"Why?"

"Bullets and shit still in me."

"I'm sorry, Carter."

He stared at me for a second, his eyes trying to focus. "Why? Did you shoot me?"

"No. But I got you into this."

He swallowed again and grunted. "Shut up, dude. You didn't do anything."

"You knew Costilla was bad news. Liz told me stay away. I didn't listen to either of you."

Carter looked at each of his arms, then the tube in his chest. "I look like a giant slurpee, bunch of fucking straws in me."

"Carter, I'm sorry," I said, a mixture of worry and guilt churning inside of me.

He wheezed a little and looked at me again. "Noah?"

"What?"

"Shut up."

I figured I could badger him with my guilt another time. "Okay."

He shut his eyes. "Know who it was yet?"

"No. Liz was here last night. They have the one I hit, but nobody else yet."

"He talking?"

"Not as of last night. But Ken Crier told me a few things."

He opened his eyes and shifted his head in my direction. "Like what?"

I told him about the heroin and Randall.

"Jesus," he said when I finished. "Kate was moving in different circles, huh?"

"I guess."

"You gonna go see Randall?"

"Yup," I said, his name lighting a fire in my gut.

"Can't it wait till I'm out?" he said, trying to smile. "I'd love to get a piece of that guy."

"You know me," I told him. "I'm impatient. And little pieces might be all that's left when I'm done with him."

He started to laugh, changed it to a grunt, suddenly looking exhausted.

The door to the room opened and a nurse informed us that it was time for me to go, as Carter needed to be prepped for surgery.

I stood. "I'll be back this afternoon."

"Good. Bring me some beer and a burrito."

I glanced at the nurse by the door, the stern look on her face saying not a chance.

I looked back at Carter. "I'll see what I can do."

I headed toward the door.

"Noah?"

I stopped. "Yeah?"

He squeezed one eye shut, kept the other bloodshot eye on me. "Kick his ass."

 30

I called the La Valencia Hotel from my cell phone, but got no answer at Randall's hotel room. I drove into La Jolla, parked on Ivanhoe, grabbed a bagel from a deli, and sat on the curb across the street from the hotel.

I kept running my conversation with Ken over in my head, trying to put the pieces together so that they fit a little more snugly. The biggest missing piece was figuring out why Kate would cover for Randall. I couldn't find a reason to take a hit like that for someone, particularly if their marriage was already imploding.

The other question that bothered me was where Kate had gone after the DEA lost her in Tijuana. She'd been missing for seventy-two hours when I'd found her. What had Costilla's men done with her in that time? It was simple to assume that Costilla's men had killed her. But the one thing that stuck in my head was that leaving her body in Mexico would have been much easier, and harder to find. Why bring her back over to the United States?

I finished the bagel and tugged on that thought until Randall appeared, walking up the other side of Prospect. His plaid short-sleeve button down, white shorts, and tan boat shoes were standard issue if you were going for a walk in La Jolla.

I crossed the street quickly and cut him off before he reached the hotel.

He didn't look happy to see me. "What the hell do you want?"

"A small bag of heroin. Got any on you?"

The blood drained from his face, and he took a step back.

"Guess not," I said. "Then I guess a private conversation with you will have to do for now."

"I'm not talking to you," he said, trying to regain his composure.

I slipped my gun out of the back of my shorts and held it casually in front of me. "Then I'm going to shoot you."

He took another step back, but I grabbed him by the shirt and pulled him toward me, jamming the barrel of the gun into his stomach.

"Choose," I said, our faces inches apart. "Right now. Talk or get shot."

Randall was a big guy who I'd managed to reduce to a little puddle of fear. I hated him for it.

"Okay," he said, trying to catch his breath. "Talk. I'll talk."

I slipped the gun back into my waistband, and we walked into the hotel and took the elevator up to his room. He pressed himself up against the far wall of the enclosed space as we rode. I stared at him.

His room was at the top, a magnificent view of the ocean out his window and balcony. The room was bright and large. A wet bar stood in one corner, and Randall went over to it.

"Drink?" he asked.

"No," I said, standing in front of the doors to the balcony in case he wanted to throw himself over it. If he got any wild ideas, like trying to charge at me, I knew I had enough space between us to draw my gun.

He dropped some ice cubes into a glass and poured four fingers of Scotch over the ice. He sucked half of it down immediately, then took a deep breath. "Okay."

"Why did Kate take the hit for you?" I asked.

He swirled the ice and alcohol in his glass. "What hit?"

I grabbed the small digital clock off the nightstand, ripped the plug out of the wall, and fired it at him.

He ducked and it sailed over his left shoulder, smashing against the wall.

He came up, flushed. "Jesus!"

"I talked to Ken," I said, the anger and frustration pouring out of me. "He explained to me exactly what kind of piece of shit you are." I walked toward him. "You wanna drag this out? Fine. I will keep throwing things at you until you tell me what the hell was going on."

He took a step back and bumped into the counter behind him. His eyes were twitchy and he looked like he was trying to make a decision.

He set his drink down. "Kate covered for me."

"I know that. Why?"

"Because I made her."

We stood there, staring at one another, his words hanging in the air between us.

"How?" I asked, resisting the urge to hit Randall as hard as I could.

Randall took a deep breath, looking nervous and pale. "I'd already had a run-in with . . . the police. I couldn't afford another. I'm sure Ken told you that."

I didn't say anything.

"She was using again," he said, shifting his weight from his right foot to his left. "Not enough for others to catch on, but just enough to stay in the groove. I told her if she didn't cover for me, I'd tell Ken and Marilyn that she was off the wagon."

I just looked at him, wondering what Kate had ever seen in him.

"She didn't want them to know," he said. "Disappointing them was always her biggest fear." He smirked over the glass at me. "I think you learned that firsthand, though, didn't you?"

I took another step forward and Randall nearly dropped his glass. It wasn't as good as punching him, but it would have to do for the moment.

"She knew they'd insist on rehab again and there

was no way she was gonna do that crap again," Randall said after a moment, his cocky bravado still there, but toned down a bit. "It was either help me or deal with her parents. I knew she'd choose me."

"So you blackmailed her," I said.

He shrugged. "I prefer to think of it as taking advantage of the situation, but you're probably right." Randall emptied his drink and poured another. "She always helped me out of my problems."

I tried to stay under control. "She didn't at the hospital."

He smiled at the glass. "No, that was one she couldn't fix. That was all mine."

I stayed quiet, not letting him off the hook.

"I went to the hospital, coming off a weekend binge," he said, settling back against the counter. "It was a mistake. We'd been high all weekend. Almost operated on a patient before somebody stepped in."

"Shouldn't you have been arrested?"

"Absolutely," he said. "No doubt. At the very least, fired. But I have a great attorney. Hospitals and insurance groups are very frightened of good attorneys."

He said it so matter-of-factly that it couldn't have been a lie.

"I was admonished," he said, rolling his eyes. "Written up. Warned that if it happened again, I was done." He paused, looking like he was trying to remember the scene. "When she got stopped, she didn't know it was in the car. So I gave her the choice. Take the blame and tell your parents the truth, that it was mine. Or tell the cops the truth and deal with everything I would tell Ken and Marilyn."

I tried to picture Kate and what she might've been thinking. Maybe it was a last-ditch attempt to save her marriage, no matter how perverse in its thinking. As I stood in the room with her husband, I became certain that he was nowhere near worth the effort she had made.

Or perhaps she simply couldn't stomach the thought of disappointing her parents again.

"Ken set the deal up," he continued. "I wasn't implicated. It seemed like it would work out fine."

"Sending your wife into a foreign country with the guy who controls the drug corridors between the U.S. and Mexico seemed fine?" I asked, my voice rising. "You seriously thought that?"

He finished off the second drink and set the empty glass on the counter. "They assured us she would be completely protected. The DA, the police, the DEA agents all told us that she wouldn't be in any danger."

"Famous last words."

He folded his arms across his chest. "They made it sound like she'd never be alone, never without protection." He paused. "Kate wasn't afraid."

That I believed. The Kate I had known was fearless. Try anything once. Live for the moment.

"After the first time, we relaxed," he said, his voice straining a bit. "She said it was fairly easy. Everyone was friendly. There were guns, but she said it was like being in a bank. A little security, but very professional."

"What did she say about Costilla?" I asked.

"Not much. Polite, friendly, somewhat intimidating, but nothing like what she expected. She said he looked like a rich businessman."

I remembered Costilla in the empty storefront in San Ysidro. Until the shooting started, I probably could have agreed with that description.

"When did you realize she was missing?" I asked.

"When the DEA called me," Randall said, his face sagging slightly. "They thought she might be with me." He stopped and rubbed his chin. "Obviously, she wasn't."

"Obviously?" I asked.

He refocused on me. "What?"

"You didn't see her after she disappeared?"

A fire started to burn in his eyes. "No, I didn't see her. And I don't think I like the implication."

I laughed. I had to. The way rich people talk can be amusing. I'm not sure that I had ever used the word "implication" in a sentence before.

"You don't, huh?" I said. "Well, let me tell you what I don't like. I don't like the fact that you are a junkie. I don't like the fact that you pulled Kate into that life with you."

"Now wait a second . . ." he said, trying to defend himself.

"I don't like the fact that you cheated on Kate," I continued, ignoring him. "I don't like the fact that you hung her out to dry because you were too much of a pussy to face it yourself. I don't like the fact that I found Kate in a car trunk. And what I really don't like, Randall, is that all of this, all of this shit, keeps curling back to you."

He stood there, his jaw set, unsure of what to say. He walked around to the bar and over to the balcony. I didn't move and he had to turn to the side to slide by me.

I turned around and watched him stand there for a moment, looking out the window. Part of me wished he would jump.

"I didn't kill Kate," he said quietly.

My head hurt. I didn't know who to believe. Randall was a manipulator and no matter how much of what he'd told me was true, I would never trust him. He'd given me no reason to.

"When Marilyn said she was hiring you," he said, turning around to face me, "she said you'd find her. She had no doubt."

"Why's that?"

A thin smile creased his lips. "She said you'd probably never gotten over her and that you'd jump at a chance to get back in touch with her."

I bit the inside of my cheek. Jump was a strong word. I had tried to resist taking the job, knowing that working for the Criers was something that would complicate my life. But, in the end, the chance to possibly see Kate again had been enough to coerce me. I hated the fact that Marilyn had been right.

"I guess this isn't what you expected," Randall said, shaking his head.

"No, it isn't," I said, clenching my teeth.

I snapped my fist into his jaw, watched him sag to the floor, and left.

 *31*

I knew Carter would still be in surgery, and since I couldn't think of any valid reason to avoid talking to Liz, I headed downtown.

My new best friend was waiting at the elevators to go up when I arrived.

"Detective," I said, resisting the urge to pat him on the head.

John Wellton, white dress shirt, red tie, gray slacks, glanced in my direction, did half a double take and scowled. "About damn time."

"For what?"

"For you to get your ass in here and do the report," he growled.

The elevator dinged, the doors opened, and we stepped in. I pushed three and he looked at me.

"How's your pal?" he asked.

"In surgery."

We stared up at the changing lights that illuminated

the floor numbers. The wheels and cables hummed, and we slowed down as we approached the third floor.

"Liz is out right now," he said, stepping off.

"Should I come back?" I asked, knowing the answer.

He grinned, shook his head, and motioned for me to follow him.

His office was across the hall from Liz's, exactly the same except that he didn't even have the calendar on the wall. He pointed to the empty chair opposite his desk. I refrained from asking if he needed a booster seat.

Wellton shuffled some papers on the desktop, then looked at me. "Liz says you're a pain in the ass, but that you'll be pretty straight up."

"I've heard that about me," I said.

He shook his head, unamused. "You're not nearly as funny as you think are. Most people aren't. Whatever. Tell me what happened."

I told him what happened. He listened intently, making a few notes every minute or so. No head nods or shakes, just sat still, listening.

"You hadn't seen the shooters before?" he asked, when I'd finished.

"No."

"Not at San Ysidro?"

"Don't know what you're talking about, Detective," I said.

He leaned back in his chair. "Fine. Off the record."

"No, they weren't there. These guys didn't look like part of Costilla's regular hitters."

He picked up a pencil and clenched it in his fist. "I'm gonna assume your friend will tell us the same story."

"Don't see why he wouldn't. It's the truth."

Wellton nodded. "Sure. Wanna know what I think?"

"Not really."

"I think Costilla's gonna kill you, Braddock," he said. "Each time you scamper away from him, you make him look bad. And he gets more pissed. You shot up his guys twice now. No way he's gonna forget you."

I let that sit in my stomach for a moment. It didn't feel good. But I knew he was right.

"That's not enough to get you off all this?" he asked, raising a dark eyebrow. "To just walk away?"

I knew it was a rhetorical question, but I answered anyway. "No, not now."

"Now?" he asked. "Why now?"

"I may have gotten his guys twice," I said, "but he put one friend in the hospital and I think he put another in the trunk of her car."

Wellton stared at me for a minute. "I guess. With your buddy in the hospital, you got others to hang with?"

I knew that he was asking if I had some other protection. "I'll be alright," I told him.

He shrugged. "Okay. But Liz's rules are still on the table. You fuck it up, we're gonna bring you in."

I stood up. "We'll see."

He grinned. "Yeah, I'm sure we will."

I turned to go.

"Braddock."

I turned around.

"Last night," he said, leaning forward, looking uncomfortable. "I didn't need to get all over you like I did, with your friend and everything."

His remark caught me off guard. "Oh. Okay. Thanks."

A flicker of a smile danced at the corner of his mouth. "But I don't trust tall suckers like you."

I didn't want to reward him with a laugh, but it was tough keeping it out of my voice. "And I'm not comfortable with anyone looking me right in the knee."

He raised his middle finger, and I waved good-bye.

 *32*

I knew that I still wouldn't be able to see Carter, which left me pondering a move that I wasn't at all thrilled with. Everything continued to point in Costilla's direction, no matter where the information came from. If I was going to truly make any progress, I was going to have to have another conversation with Alejandro Costilla.

I resisted the urge to head home and into the comfort of the waves, instead taking the long way out of downtown. I pointed the Blazer south down Harbor Drive along San Diego Bay, past the convention center, Petco Park, and the naval shipyards before making up my mind to head farther south into Chula Vista on I-5.

Yuppie suburbs were popping up in the hills of Bonita and the eastern end of Chula Vista and Otay Mesa. Million-dollar homes were the result of immense population growth in the nineties. The United States Olympic Committee had even seen fit to build a new, state-of-the-art training center in an area adjacent to Lower Otay Lake.

But the western side of Chula Vista hadn't benefited from the influx of money and people and had remained what it had always been when I was growing up—a dangerous place.

I exited at E Street and went east. Single-story box homes lined the streets, iron bars on the windows signifying the presence of the gangs that ruled the area. Some of the billboards advertised in Spanish, the cars rode lower to the ground, and the stares of the people on the sidewalks became longer and uglier.

The Enrique Camarena Recreation Center was just south of Eucalyptus Park at 4th and C and stood out like a lost child in a shopping mall. Built in honor of the slain DEA agent, the center was only about six years old, its newer brick and glass clashing with the crumbling stucco and concrete of the neighborhood that surrounded it. I parked in the lot and went inside.

An older Hispanic lady sat behind the front desk. Thick gray hair bundled on top of her head, deep lines around tired eyes, and overweight arms poking out of a purple tank top she had no business wearing.

"Help you?" she asked, her eyes barely leaving the magazine in front of her.

"Looking for Ernie," I said.

She lifted her chin in a direction that I took meant down the hall. "Second door on your right."

As I walked toward Ernie's office, I heard the squeaking of sneakers on a clean hardwood floor, along with shouts and the bouncing of a ball. I stopped at the second door and knocked.

"Yo," a voice called from behind. "Come in."

I stepped in and Ernie Romario looked at me. "You lost, Braddock?"

"Just checking up on you," I said, smiling.

"Bullshit," he said.

He stood and extended his arm across the desk. He wore white athletic shorts and a tight gray tank top that exposed lean, tattooed arms. Faces of women mostly, a couple of crosses thrown in for good measure. The black hair on his scalp was shaved down, and a barely visible goatee encircled his mouth.

We shook hands.

"Sit," he said.

The office was small. A tiny metal desk, with a chair on either side. The walls were covered with photos and articles detailing the accomplishments of the Camarena Center. Most featured kids that had used the Center as a place to hang out and then gone on to bigger and better things. Most of the photos featured those kids with Ernie and his staff.

I pointed to the pictures. "Still famous."

He shrugged his shoulders, the tattoo of an angel on his left one dancing. "The kids, brother. The kids are the famous ones."

Ernie had gone to high school with Carter, Liz, Kate, and me. His parents had gotten him transferred out of the South Bay to avoid the gangs and violence that permeated the high schools where they lived. He'd played football with Carter and me, a nasty little defensive back with a chip on his shoulder. He knew he didn't fit in at our school and that was okay. During football season, he hung with us, but when it was over, he kept to himself. He avoided the gangs in Chula Vista and San Ysidro, but didn't abandon his friends from the neighborhood. I'd always surmised that was why he decorated his body with the ink, to prove to the homies that he was still one of them, even if he wasn't.

He'd gone to State with me, majored in recreation and education, and was the first and only director that the Camarena Center had hired. He made sure that everyone was welcome, but that the violence and crap that littered the streets around the building stayed outside. Being a local, the violent little thugs that ran the neighborhood respected Ernie and what he was doing. They stayed away from the building and didn't bother those entering it.

"Don't tell me you were in the neighborhood," Ernie said, a sly grin creeping onto his face. "I know better."

"What? I can't come see my friend without reason?"

He nodded. "You could, yeah. But after what I heard about in San Ysidro, I figure you got a reason."

I shifted in the chair. "San Ysidro?"

He rolled his dark eyes. "Please, *gringo*. Two white dudes shoot a couple of *hermanos*, plus they driving something out of the junkyard. Ain't nobody that could be but you and Carter."

I shrugged. "Maybe."

Ernie leaned forward. "Maybe my ass. Dude, why are you messing with Alejandro Costilla?"

I told him about Kate and what had happened over the previous couple of days.

He tapped his fingers lightly on the desk when I was through. "Glad I'm not you."

"I get that a lot."

He nodded. "Carter gonna be alright?"

"Think so."

Ernie laughed. "Course. Gonna have to kill him for him to not be alright."

"Probably."

A couple of voices yelled at one another from a distance down the hall, then dissolved into laughter.

I gestured over my shoulder. "This place always so happy?"

"Pretty much," Ernie said after a moment. "Better than what's going on in their homes. If they got one."

"That sucks."

"Yeah, it does." Ernie laid his palms up on the desk. "Why you here, Noah?"

I folded my arms across my chest. "I need to get with Costilla."

Ernie raised both eyebrows. "Why? You want him to cut your head off?"

"I'd prefer that he not."

"That's what he's gonna do, Noah," he said. "No doubt about it."

Ernie's voice had changed, much more tense now. Like he didn't want me in his office.

"I need to see him, Ernie," I said.

He leaned back in his chair. "And you think I can get you to him?"

I nodded. "Yeah. Carter set it up before. He can't now, obviously." I paused. "You were next on the list."

He looked at me for a moment, his eyes studying me. Then he shook his head. "I don't wanna do that."

"Just need you to get me in touch with him. I don't need you to be there."

"That's good 'cause I ain't going anywhere near that man," he said. Ernie chewed on his bottom lip for a moment. "You know what happens if I help you?"

"Yeah. I get to meet with Costilla."

"Yeah, and when you don't come back and they find your arms in TJ and your legs in Rosarito and your head in El Centro, then you know what?" He stared at me. "Then I'm responsible."

"He's not gonna kill me," I said, trying to sound like I meant it.

A barking laugh burst out from Ernie's mouth. "Right. 'Cause Alejandro Costilla always makes friends. That's what the dude's all about, right? Probably just wanted to scare you guys, sending those bangers to catch you on the freeway."

I didn't know what to say because I knew Ernie was right. He knew the world I was trying to get into much better than I did. That's why I'd come to him. And I didn't see a way to figure out the whole mess without seeing Costilla.

"Ernie, I don't have a choice," I said. "He's got answers that I need. And he's gonna come after me anyway. Hell, he already has. I've got nothing to lose."

"Except your life," he said quietly.

We let that hang in the air between us for a couple of minutes. Ernie was being a friend, trying to protect me from myself, which I appreciated. The problem, though, was that I didn't need a friend. I needed a drug dealer.

"Call me tomorrow," he said finally. "Here. Eight in the morning. I can't promise anything."

I stood up. "Thanks."

Ernie stood. "Don't thank me. You may think I'm doing you a favor, but I'm not."

We shook hands.

"I know," I said.

"I don't think you do, Noah," he said. "I don't think you do."

 *33*

I left Chula Vista in a bad mood. And hungry.

I stopped at Roberto's in Ocean Beach, above Sunset Cliffs, and grabbed a burrito and some rolled tacos. As I sat at the streetside table and watched the tourists and locals mingle along Antique Row, the hunger went away, but the bad mood didn't.

I didn't feel good about putting Ernie in the position I'd left him in, but I knew it was the most direct route to Costilla. I tried to tell myself that if Ernie really hadn't wanted to help me, he wouldn't have. I knew that was a lie, though. Friends, at least my friends, helped each other out. Loyalty was high on the list for me and the people I let into my life. It was loyalty to Kate that was driving me. Not her parents' money, not anger, not even Carter getting hurt. Just loyalty. Ernie knew that if he ever came to me with something, I'd help him. A few questions asked, maybe, but I'd do it.

I just hoped I'd be around for the next time he needed me.

I drove up to UCSD and found Carter back in his hospital bed, more color in his face than when I'd left him yesterday. The frown he sported, though, was new. It seemed to be directed at what looked like fresh medical tape covering the upper part of his chest near his right arm.

"Hey," I said.

"Hey," he said, still scowling. "Feels like someone ate a piece of my shoulder."

"They give you any pain meds?"

He shook his head. "Tried to but I didn't want them."

I grabbed the chair by the window and slid it closer to the bed. "Well, that's dumb."

"My body is a temple."

I spun the chair around and straddled it backward. "Your body is more like an all-night rave."

"Whatever. I don't want to be doped up." He shifted slightly on the bed. "So, where you been?"

"Went to see Ernie."

He fiddled with the IV tube that tucked into the back of his left hand. "I hope you mean the *Sesame Street* guy."

"No, that Bert fella can be a real pain in the ass."

The frown returned. "If you went to see Ernie, that means you are going to do something pretty stupid."

I shrugged.

"Do I want to know?" he asked.

"No."

He shifted again in the bed, and all of the tubes running out of his body shivered. "If you're doing what I think you're doing, at least let me know when. That way I'll know what to tell the cops when you disappear."

I didn't want to talk about Costilla, even with Carter. Too much was going on in my head, and I didn't want to share it until I had organized it.

"Saw Emily last night," I said, switching to a subject I knew he'd be interested in.

"Saw Emily last night or saw Emily last night and this morning?" he asked, a tired smile forcing its way onto his mouth.

"The first one."

He tugged at the tubes entering his nose, adjusting them. "Glad to know my hospitalization hasn't hindered your love life."

"It's not a love life."

"Sex life?"

"Nothing happened, and I don't know what it is."

"Does she?"

"Does she what?" I asked.

"Does she have an idea of what it is?" Carter said. "Or what she wants it to be?"

I shook my head. "We haven't talked about it."

"Are you going to?"

I shrugged because I didn't know the answer. Half of me felt like Emily and I were gravitating toward one another out of grief. That would be understandable.

But the other half of me wondered if maybe there was more to it. Maybe in a twisted sense, I was getting a second chance. And I wasn't sure if I wanted it.

"You'll figure it out," Carter said.

"Probably," I said.

The door to the room opened and a nurse hurried in with a green tray. The food was covered. She set it across his lap and disappeared out the door.

"It's covered because that way I can't tell her it sucks when she drops it off," he said.

I laughed. "I'll see if I can't get you some decent dinner in here tonight."

He lifted the various covers, unveiling some sort of chicken and jello combination. "Yeah, be a pal." He poked at the food with the fork. "I was thinking about what you told me. About Kate and Randall."

"Oh yeah?"

"His alleged affairs. You think whoever he was messing with was into the drugs, too?"

I hadn't connected those two avenues. "I don't know."

"Might be interesting to find out where that heroin Kate had in the car with her came from," he said.

Randall had said it was his, but hadn't told me where it had come from. In my anger, I had neglected to ask some important questions.

"Yeah, it might," I said.

Carter forked some of the dark red jello. "I'm just thinking that if he was sleeping with somebody else who shared their habit, Kate might've known her, too."

"And if there was some friction there, we may have somebody else who had a reason to kill Kate," I said.

He sucked the jello off the fork and aimed the empty utensil at me. "Bingo."

I stood up. "Watching you eat that is making me sick."

"I'm already sick so how do you think I feel?"

"Not good," I said, walking to the door. "I'll try and get back tonight."

"Noah?"

I turned. "Yeah?"

"I'm serious," Carter said, his eyes confirming that statement. "If you're going to see Costilla, I want to know when."

"Yes, Mom."

"Call me mommy, daddy, or granny," he said. "I don't care. But let me know."

Somewhere in the back of my head, it occurred to me that he might try to drag himself out of the hospital to accompany me, tubes and all. I couldn't let him do that.

"I will," I lied and left.

 *34*

I thought about calling Emily, Liz, and Randall, all for different reasons, but couldn't get motivated about any of those options. I avoided doing all three, ordered Chinese, and listened to the Padres get pounded by the Dodgers on the radio out on the patio.

Sleep came in spurts, in between thinking about Kate and the guilt of avoiding Emily and lying to Carter. I got out of bed at six, found a few good waves near the jetty, and rode those for about an hour, then came back and showered and dialed Ernie at eight on the nose.

"Couldn't wait, huh?" he said when he answered the phone.

"Yeah. Just too excited."

"Jesus," he said. "You're ridiculous."

"I know."

"Well, that's something at least." I heard papers moving on his desk. "You got a pen?"

I fished one off the coffee table. "Yeah."

"You know the Cultural Plaza in TJ?"

"Sure."

"Be there at noon," he said. "Then call this number." He read me an unfamiliar number. "Let it ring twice, then hang up. Someone will come and get you."

"Then what?" I asked.

"I got no idea, Noah," he said, his voice indicating that he didn't want to know either. "I'd tell you to take some help, but I doubt you'd get to him if you did."

"Don't worry. I'll be fine."

"I could probably go," Ernie offered. "They might let me go with you."

"No," I said quickly, before I could change my mind. "I don't want you to do that."

We both knew what I was implying. If something was going to happen, I wanted it to happen to me, not Ernie.

"I owe you," I told him.

"Damn straight," he replied. "Make sure you get back to pay up." He hung up.

I stared at the number Ernie had given me, unsure of where it was going to lead me. I was indebted to him because he'd gone out on a limb to get me the information I needed. His board of directors would probably frown on the ease with which he was able to arrange a meeting with Alejandro Costilla.

I spent the next two hours picking up my place, trying to burn the nervous energy that was slowly building in my body. The house was spic-and-span when I left a little after ten.

I drove to the outlets where Carter and I had met Costilla for the first time. The dirt lots that sit across from the stores serve as free parking for those walking across the border. After five minutes of deliberation, I slid my gun under the seat and locked up the rented SUV.

Walking the hundred or so yards across the border feels no different than walking a hundred or so yards in any other place. Small children offer to sell you gum, old women sit stonelike on the sidewalk presiding over handmade jewelry, and Americans walk south in droves. You simply walk through a fence and under an overpass and you're in another country.

The taxi drivers swarm as soon as you cross, though. A thin, younger man waved at me, raised his eyebrows. I nodded. He spun and opened the door of a beat-up, dusty white Ford Escort. He shut it behind me and hustled to the driver's seat.

"Where you go, sir?" he said, smiling in the rearview mirror. "Revolución?"

I shook my head at his mention of the area of nightclubs that most Americans sought out. "No. The Cultural Center in the Plaza."

He gave a quick nod. "*Sí.*"

He followed the other taxis as they pulled away from the sidewalk in a cloud of dust. The entry roads at the border crossing are dirty and bumpy, but after about a five-minute ride, you are on streets and highways that are indistinguishable from those on the American side, save for much less traffic.

The Plaza is fifteen minutes from the border but we made it there in about ten. The taxi pulled into the traffic circle and slowed to a halt.

The driver turned around. "This good?"

"Yeah," I said, pulling a twenty from my wallet and handing it to him. "Thanks."

He took the bill, nodded with a big smile, and gave a small wave.

I hoped that Liz or the DEA would not be interviewing him in the next few days as potentially the last person to have seen Noah Braddock alive. At least they'd know I tipped well, though.

The Cultural Center is in the newer, more modern section of TJ, and for the most part looks very similar to what you might see in the downtown area of a mid-sized American city. The main building is a museum, showcasing the history of the Baja California peninsula. A fountain is the centerpiece of the outdoor plaza, with families carrying shopping bags, vendors selling ice cream and drinks, and picnics on the grass.

I walked around the fountain for a moment, looking for a phone, the mist from the water cooling me off in the afternoon heat. I had just spotted one when I felt a gun barrel dig into my ribs.

"Mr. Braddock," a voice said in my ear. "Good to see you."

I turned sideways awkwardly and recognized Ramon. "Can't say the same."

"Do I need the gun?" he asked.

"No."

The gun eased out of my back, and I turned a little more to see him.

Ramon wore gray linen slacks and a tight black T-shirt. The same hard eyes reminded me of why I'd been wary of him before.

"Where we headed?" I asked.

He pointed to a silver Mercedes slowing in the traffic circle. "Right there."

"And then?"

He laughed as we walked toward the car. He opened the rear passenger door for me, and I got in.

Two men I didn't recognize were staring at me from the front seat. The driver had a fat head, shaved bald, and eyes that were almost swallowed up by his chubby cheeks. His partner sported a tight crew cut of black hair, bright green eyes, and a sweaty upper lip. Neither smiled.

Ramon slid in next to me. "Go."

The two men turned around, and the car started to move.

Ramon produced a blindfold that looked like one of those sleep masks people wear in hotels.

"I'd appreciate it if you'd put this on," he said.

"If I don't?"

He smiled. "I'd appreciate it if you'd put this on. Yourself."

I took the mask from him and slipped it on over my eyes. Tiny slivers of light slithered under the mask at the bottom of my eyes, but everything else was black.

I adjusted to riding in the dark and tried to listen for

sounds that might give me an idea of where we were headed. The only thing I could make out was the hum of the air conditioning and the constant whir of the wheels on the road.

We rode in silence for what I thought I calculated to be about an hour, but I knew that my sense of time was tenuous because of the silence and lack of vision.

The car slowed to a stop, the tires crunching over gravel.

"Please remove the mask," Ramon said.

I did, and the light felt violent and unfriendly.

 **35**

I stepped out of the Mercedes, Ramon behind me. We were at the bottom of a small grassy hill. A dirt trail bisected the slope to the top. I looked around and saw nothing else. A small mountain in the middle of a field that looked as if it extended for miles in every direction. I couldn't even tell which way we'd driven in from.

"I need to check you," Ramon said.

I stood still and extended my arms. He patted me down quickly and efficiently, finishing at my ankles. He was better than most cops.

He stood up. "Follow the trail to the top."

I turned and headed up the trail. It looked to be about three hundred yards, a gradual ascent that wasn't too taxing. I turned around once to see Ramon standing at the bottom of the trailhead, watching me.

About midway, I could see the ocean out in the distance to the west. The field and hill were actually on top of a bluff, maybe half a mile from the coast. In Southern California, it would've been prime real estate, developed to the hilt. Here, it was simply a pretty piece of land.

I reached the top and found Alejandro Costilla waiting for me, sitting on a wooden bench, facing me. He wore white cotton pants and a long-sleeve burgundy dress shirt. I could see a small gold cross at the base of his neck. He was surrounded by three men, all dressed in shorts and T-shirts, all aiming machine guns at me.

Costilla gestured in my direction. "Check him."

The one to his left stepped forward, slung the gun to his back, and patted me down, just as Ramon had done.

"Ramon cleared me already," I said.

Costilla said nothing. The man finished patting me down, then nodded quickly in Costilla's direction. He backed away from me, returning to his original spot, his gun again pointed at me.

"I'm surprised you came," Costilla said.

"Needed to see you."

He rose from the bench. "You don't think I'm going to kill you?" he asked, shoving his hands in his pockets.

I wasn't sure how to answer that, so I was honest. "I have no idea. I hope not."

He smiled. "Good to have hope. How is your friend?"

"Alive," I said. "How is your man?"

"Alive," he said. "You know, it was supposed to be you that ended up in the hospital. Or the grave."

"Figured that," I said.

He laughed, shaking his head. "You've got balls, Mr. Braddock. Bigger than your brain, probably."

I shrugged.

He extended his arms out to the sides, palms up. "So here I am. What is it you want to talk to me about?"

I felt isolated on the hill, probably as they intended. If they were going to kill me, there was nothing I could do about it. I figured I should at least try to get what I came for.

"Are you responsible for Kate Crier's death?" I asked.

"You are still working on this? Even after I told you to stop?" Costilla looked incredulous.

"Yeah."

"And now you think I killed this girl?"

"I think it's a possibility."

He smiled, squinting into the sun. "And if I tell you I did, what are you going to do?" He waved his arm around. "What are you going to do to me?"

There was nothing I could do at that moment and he knew it, too. I didn't say anything.

He shook his head and ran a hand over his bald scalp. "You think I killed your friend because she was working for your government?"

"So you did know what she was doing," I said, his statement confirming my guess.

"Of course," he said, as if only a moron wouldn't have known. "I knew immediately."

"How?"

He frowned. "You think I've gotten to this point

without being smart? Without being careful? No one gets close to me without my knowing who they are." He shook his head again. "You disappoint me, Mr. Braddock."

A knot formed in my stomach, and I couldn't untangle it. I waited for him to continue.

Costilla walked back to the bench and sat, leaning back on his hands and crossing his outstretched legs at the ankles. "I didn't kill her."

That surprised me. He had no reason to lie to me. I was at his mercy. I thought he would enjoy telling me about her death, how he'd done it and how he was happy she was gone. And how I was next.

"But you knew what she was doing," I said. "That she was an informant."

He nodded. "Yes, I did. I made a mistake the last time your government tried to get inside my people. I killed that person."

It wasn't making sense. "Why was that a mistake?"

His head gleamed in the sun. "Let me ask you a question. Let's say you are trying to hide from someone. That someone tries to get information about where you are going to hide."

"Okay," I said.

"Tell me, is it easier to just try and hide or to give that someone information that might make them look elsewhere?" He raised his eyebrows. "Send them looking in places where you aren't."

Now I was getting it. "So you fed Kate bad information?"

"Ask your police friends," he said, laughing. "Ask them how they like looking for ghosts."

"They wired her," I said, still not entirely believing him.

He rolled his eyes. "Naturally. Ask them about what they heard, if anything they heard helped them catch me." He looked at himself, mocking. "Oh, wait. Here I am."

I don't know how one comes to trusting someone that can't be trusted, but there was no doubt in my mind that Alejandro Costilla was telling the truth.

 **36**

"Do you know who killed her then?" I asked.

Costilla pointed a finger at me. "Therein lies the problem, Mr. Braddock."

"I don't get it," I said, shaking my head.

He stood and motioned for me to walk to the edge of the plateau with him. I looked at the men and their guns, hoped they weren't going to shoot me, then joined Costilla where he stood.

"I don't know who killed her," he said, gazing out in the distance toward the ocean. "If I did, I would've already taken care of it."

"Mr. Costilla, I don't understand a word of what you're telling me," I said.

He dropped his hands back into his pockets. "Ms. Crier had something that belonged to me."

"Drugs?"

"Money," he said, turning to me. "Half a million dollars."

The knot in my stomach tightened.

"Now, of course, it's not the amount that mattered to me," he continued. "Rather a small amount when you look at the big picture. But it was mine and she took it."

"You're certain it was her?"

He nodded. "Yes. And even though I am not the one that killed her, I would have if I'd found her first. I can't tolerate people stealing from me."

The knot felt cold in my stomach. Kate had managed to operate in Costilla's world without getting herself killed, even though the man she was informing on knew who she was. Now he was telling me that she stole from him and he'd planned to do what someone else had already done.

"Why'd she steal the money?" I asked. "There's no way she'd think she could get that past you and her handlers."

He rubbed his chin. "I've wondered that, too. But I don't know why she did it. Maybe she was going to try and outrun me and her government." He smiled. "Brave girl."

"Yeah," I said. "Brave."

"When I told you I wanted you to stop looking into this," he said, "it was because I wanted to find my money. I figured, you or your police find it, I lose it. And also because I will kill whoever took my money and killed our friend."

"I don't think she was your friend," I said.

Costilla shrugged. "No, but she was useful to me.

Her death inconvenienced me and disrupted my plans. That doesn't please me." He paused, then turned to look at me. "I think I misjudged you, however."

"How's that?"

"I figured, if you were trying to solve all this, you would turn in the person that killed your friend," he said. "But now I see something different."

His observation irritated me. "You don't know me."

"True, but I know it when I see it," he said.

"See what?"

"Someone looking for revenge," he said and smiled.

We stood there for a moment, looking at one another, remaining silent. I didn't like his trying to get in my head. Or the fact that he might have been right.

"You beat up one of my men, you shoot another," he said. "You come here to meet with me after your friend is hurt. These are things someone does only if he is dumb or determined. And you, Mr. Braddock, are not dumb. I am confident of that."

I looked away from him. I knew that what he was saying, what he saw in me, was the truth.

"So where does that leave us?" I asked.

He rocked on his heels, jingling some change in his pockets. "I'm going to let you keep looking." He grinned at me. "I know, you didn't need my permission. Whatever. I think you are the person who will figure it out. The way I see it, the person that killed your friend has my money."

"You think I'm going to get you your money back?"

He shook his head. "No, it's clear to me that you

would not do such a thing. I thought at first, maybe. But I'm not going to waste either of our time by suggesting that." He looked at me. "But I'll be watching you."

"So I can take you to your money?" I said.

Costilla shrugged. "Perhaps. But to be honest, I just want to see if I'm right."

"Right about what?"

He looked at me, his eyes cold and hard like the first day I'd met him in San Ysidro. "To see if you are going to kill this person. Because I think, from what I see, you are."

"You a psychology major?" I asked, again irritated with his analysis of me.

"No, but you are working in my area now," he said, smiling again. He rubbed his scalp. "Now, we have one more thing to attend to."

"We do?"

He nodded. "Yes. When I said that I was going to find your friend after she stole my money, you understand why?"

"I think so," I said. "Doesn't look good to have someone show you up."

He pointed at me. "Exactly. Yesterday, on the freeway, you and your friend showed me up."

The knot that had been in my stomach doubled in size.

"I can't have that," he said quietly. He turned and waved over my shoulder.

I turned around to see Ramon and my other two escorts approaching us. They passed the armed men and stood in front of me.

"I'm not going to kill you, Mr. Braddock," Alejandro Costilla said. "I actually like you. And it's easier for me if you take care of your friend's murder. I get to watch and cheer you on. So I'm not going to kill you." He paused and stepped closer to me, his mouth right next to my ear. "But it might feel like you are going to die."

The driver's hand shot out toward my chest. I managed to knock it away and drove the palm of my hand into his nose. A fist caught me in the temple, and my vision blurred. Another exploded into my kidneys, and I fell to my knees.

I stayed there for a moment, trying to catch my breath, trying to fight the reds and purples that were swirling in my eyes. Something cold and hard smashed into the back of my head, and the colors changed from red to yellow to white and, finally, to black.

 **37**

I came back slowly to the world, feeling as if the car that had run over me was still parked squarely on my body.

I tried to open my eyes, but they felt like they were sealed shut. I tried to sit up, but could only manage a groan that sounded distant and ugly, as my body rattled with pain.

"Noah?" a voice said. "You awake?"

I forced my right eye open and made out a fuzzy image of Ernie. I groaned again.

"You awake?" he asked again.

I brought my hand up to my eyes and rubbed them, slowly opening the other. Ernie came into focus.

"Ernie?" I said, my throat dry and raw.

"Yeah, it's me, dumbass. How you feel?"

My arms felt heavy, my legs felt like lead, my back ached, and my head throbbed.

"Alright," I mumbled. I cleared my throat. "Where am I?"

"My house," he said. "Somebody called me, told me where to find you."

I blinked my eyes, then tried to sit up. A fire roared up my spine and into the back of my head. I fell back down.

"Easy," Ernie said. He was sitting on a chair and I was on a bed.

"Where was I?"

"Out on the beach in IB," he said, shaking his head. "I guess they dropped you there when they were finished."

Slowly, I remembered that I'd gone to see Costilla. I remembered the conversation.

"Imperial Beach?" I said. "I thought we were in TJ."

He shrugged. "I don't know. I got a call. You were where they said you would be, by the pier."

I tried to sit up again, held still as my head caught fire, and managed to make it up to a hunched-over position. Ernie handed me a glass of water.

"Thanks," I said, sipping it. "How do I look?"

"Like somebody kicked the shit out of you," he said, shaking his head. "But I gotta say, I was wrong. I thought they'd kill you. But somehow you made it back."

I nodded, drinking more of the water. I knew that the only reason I was alive was because Costilla had wanted it that way. He easily could've fulfilled Ernie's prediction.

"I called Liz," Ernie said.

I felt my eyes widen. "What? Why?"

"I didn't know what else to do," he said. "Carter's in the hospital, he can't help. I figured you didn't want to go to the hospital. You told me you'd been talking to Liz about all of this."

What I'd forgotten to mention was that I wasn't supposed to go see Costilla.

"What did you tell her?"

He frowned. "That I dug you up off the beach after Costilla had pummeled you."

"You said it was Costilla?"

"Yeah."

"Shit," I said. I swung my legs over the edge of the bed, invisible spikes digging into the backs of my thighs. "Help me up."

"Whoa, dude," Ernie said, putting a hand on my shoulder. "You are in no shape to go anywhere."

"Liz on her way?" I asked.

"Yeah."

"Then help me up."

"Why?"

"Because I gotta take off before she arrives."

I pushed up off the bed and stood slowly. I felt like I had parts where they weren't supposed to be and an awful case of the flu.

"Noah, you told me Liz knows what's going on," Ernie said, confused.

I braced myself on the back of his chair. "What I didn't tell you was that I'm not allowed anywhere near Costilla."

He looked at me, then realized what I was getting at. "Aw, Jesus. I'm sorry."

I waved a hand at him. "Not your fault. You didn't know. Help me to the bathroom."

He hunched forward and I put my arm around his shoulders and we slowly made our way to the bathroom. I was encouraged that nothing seemed to be broken. The small things in life.

I stood in front of the sink and turned on the faucet. My reflection in the mirror didn't scare me as much as I'd anticipated. A small cut over my right eye and a bruise on each cheek. Dried blood at the corner of my mouth. Most of the damage had been done to my legs and torso. I lifted up my shirt. Reds, pinks, and purples dominated my ribs and back.

"You can take a punch, I'll say that," Ernie said.

I grunted at him. I cupped my hands under the cold water and brought them up to my face. The water shocked me, and my head started to clear. I rinsed my face a couple more times and wiped my face with the towel hanging on the wall.

Ernie reached into the mirrored medicine cabinet on the wall next to us. He pulled out a bottle of aspirin and shook four out and handed them to me.

I swallowed the pills, drank another handful of water, and shut off the faucet.

Leaning gingerly against the sink, I said, "My car's at the border. Can you take me?"

"You sure you can drive?" Ernie asked.

"I'll be fine. I'm sorry I got you into this. Get me to my car and I'll be out of your hair."

"And you'll owe me."

"Big time," I said.

He offered his shoulders again, but I waved him off. If I was going to drive, I'd better walk first. I limped behind him. I felt more awake, but I felt the swelling and bruising a little more, too. I silently pleaded with the aspirin to kick in.

Ernie led me through the single-story bungalow that he owned. It was a couple of blocks from the youth center. He'd bought it a couple of years ago, saying that he wanted to live in the neighborhood he worked in. It would've been dangerous for a guy like me to move into the neighborhood, but for Ernie, it was like the mayor living among his constituents.

As he reached for the door, a knock came from the other side of it.

He turned and looked at me.

I had momentary thoughts of looking for the back door, hopping a fence, and trying to get the hell out of there. Then I realized how long it had taken us to get from the bathroom to the front door.

"It's okay," I said. "Let her in."

He opened the door and Liz stood there, glaring at us. In black slacks and a black blouse, she looked like a hot, female version of the Grim Reaper.

"Gentlemen," she said. "Going somewhere?"

"No," I croaked. "We were just both so anxious to see you."

"Right," she said. "And you look great, by the way."

"I know."

Ernie stood between us, unsure of what his role was. I looked at him. "Thanks."

"Anytime," he said, and I knew that he meant it.

I pushed open the screen door and limped out onto the porch. I looked at Liz. "You gonna cuff me?"

She put her hand behind my elbow to steady me and help me to her car. "No, you don't look like you can do much damage right now."

"Exactly," I said. "So why arrest me?"

"Because it gives me pleasure to Mirandize you," she said.

Then she read me my rights.

 **38**

Liz let me ride in the front seat.

"You're really gonna do this?" I asked, as we zipped up I-5, passing the Mile of Cars exit in National City.

"Yeah," she said, without looking at me. "I am."

I shifted in the seat, a new wave of aches and pains surging through my body. "Maybe I should go to the hospital."

"You look fine to me."

"You're not looking at me."

"Well, then, you sound fine to me."

I could see the anger in her face and in her body language. She'd told me what would happen if I went near Costilla again and apparently she was going to follow through on her promise to sit me in jail. I wasn't pleased with that idea, but I knew that I was making her job harder. Not only because of what I was doing, but also because of who I was. I knew that her fellow officers were probably enjoying the fact that her ex-boyfriend was screwing up her investigation.

"I'm sorry," I said.

"No, you're not, Noah," she said. "You're never sorry."

"Well, this time I am."

"Whoop-de-doo."

We passed the old Rohr Industries plant, across the way from where Ernie said he'd found me. I hadn't gotten a chance to ask him more about the phone call he'd received and how to find me. It was starting to sink in how lucky I was to be alive.

"I got some information," I said.

"I could not care less."

"I don't believe that."

"I told you not to go near Costilla," she said, glancing at me, her disgust apparent. "You ignored me. And now I'm the one taking shit for it."

I felt the car speed up, her anger moving into the gas pedal.

"I had to go see him, Liz," I told her.

"No, you didn't," she shot back. "You needed to talk to me first."

"Why? So you could've told me to stay away again?"

She shook her head. "Look, I didn't bust you on San Ysidro or the thing with Carter and leaving the scene. In fact, I defended you and kept everybody off of you. And in return you go behind my back and do the one thing I asked you not to do."

It was like being chastised by a parent.

It worked.

"Sorry," I mumbled.

"Whatever," she said, waving a hand in the air, ending the conversation.

We drove the rest of the way to the station in silence. She cuffed me loosely before we got out of the car and helped me up the stairs to the building.

She took me down a flight of stairs, past the processing office, and waved at a short, thick uniformed officer at a desk. He stood quickly and walked with us. We made a couple of turns until we came to a quiet hallway with several empty cells.

"What are you charging me with?" I asked.

"Being an asshole," Liz said. "You've been guilty for a long time."

The officer stopped in front of the first cell and unlocked it as Liz removed my handcuffs.

"You can't just keep me here."

"Watch me."

"I get a phone call then," I said, as the guard opened the empty cell.

Liz nodded. "In a little bit."

She put her hand in the small of my back and guided me in.

"Not in a little bit," I said. "Now."

The cell door clanged shut, and I turned around. Liz had her hands wrapped around the outside of the bars. She nodded to the guard, and he disappeared down the hall.

"I'll get you your phone call," she said. "How about you tell me what you think you learned."

"You wanna let me out of here?"

"Not particularly," she said, smiling. "This is the most attractive you've looked to me in a long time."

"Then screw you."

"You did that and it wasn't much to rave about," she said, the smile getting wider. She was clearly enjoying this position. "You don't wanna talk then?"

I shook my head slowly.

She shrugged. "Fine with me."

Standing in a jail cell to call my own, I felt dumb, frustrated, and tired. Her explanation of what she'd let me get away with to this point had hit home. I'd been way outside the lines and she'd basically covered for me. I'd made her look bad by getting near Costilla again. I couldn't blame her for being angry with me.

She turned to go.

"He knew, Liz," I said.

She stopped. "Who?"

"Costilla."

"He knew what?"

I turned and walked over to the bench next to the wall and sat down gingerly. She may have been right, but it didn't mean I liked being locked up.

"You figure it out," I said.

I heard her shoes click down the hallway.

 *39*

"Braddock. Get up."

The voice startled me, and I opened my eyes. I'd laid down on the bench and dozed off. As I tried to sit up, the stiffness in my joints and muscles slowed me. If the aspirin Ernie had given me had kicked in, I wasn't feeling it.

Detective John Wellton was standing outside the cell. He wore an olive-green dress shirt, tan slacks, and a silver tie.

"Having a good time?" he asked.

"The best." I managed to push myself to an upright position, but my back was arguing that it wasn't a great idea. "Where's Liz?"

"Trying to explain to the lieutenant why she's got a private dick locked up down here with no charges filed," he said, frowning.

"Am I out of here then?" I asked.

"In a minute," he said, leaning back against the bars

of the cell behind him. "Listen to me for a second, okay?"

"No thanks."

"I don't know what's between you and Liz," he said anyway. "And I could give a shit. But she's covering your ass left and right and seems to care that you don't die. Me, I think it would be easier if you were dead."

I stood up and walked awkwardly over to the front of the cell.

"And you know what she gets for all her hard work? Nothing. A fucking headache, maybe, but not much else," Wellton said. "You run around, pretending to be a tough guy and all, and she ends up picking up behind you. She wants the same thing you do."

"And what's that?"

He stepped toward my cell door. "To find out who killed your friend, you dumbass. You think she doesn't feel guilty about what happened to her? You think it's not keeping her up at night? Jesus. Everyone keeps telling me you're a pain in the ass but a smart guy. Well, I see the first part, but I have yet to see the second."

His words hung between us, as heavy as the iron bars I was holding on to.

"Why do you care?" I asked, not having anything else to say that seemed worthwhile. "I mean, about her."

"Because she's my friend," he said. "And she's my partner. You think it's easy being partnered with a black guy the size of a sixth grader? She's never said shit about it and never taken any shit from anyone about it. I mean, they tried to give her shit, but she wouldn't have any of it." He paused, staring at me. "I'd go to the wall for her because I know she'd go at least that far for me."

I slowly began to feel like that guy in the cartoon where his head morphs into that of a jackass. I could feel the buck teeth and long ears sprouting.

"Get her," I said. "I'll tell her what I know."

Wellton pointed at me. "Goddamn right you will. And then you'll stay the hell out of her way. And mine. Because if you don't, I'm going to make it so that the only thing I care about is seeing you go down."

He stalked away, his angry footsteps echoing down the hall.

 *40*

A guard came to the cell and escorted me to a conference room down the hall from the cells. I sat there for about fifteen minutes, staring at my hands, before Liz came in.

"Before we start, I want to get something straight," she said, sitting down in the chair on the other side of the table. "If you want to play around, I don't—"

I held my hand up, interrupting her. "I'm done messing around. I promise."

She studied me for a moment. "You just said you promised."

I nodded. "I did. And I mean it."

"Yeah," she said, leaning back in the chair. "I know you do."

When it comes to women, I'm admittedly not too hot in the communication department. I don't especially like to talk about serious things or philosophical situations. They make me uncomfortable. When Liz and I were together and we did talk about those things, Liz sometimes doubted whether I was being honest with her. When she wanted the truth out of me, she made me say, "I promise." I had never once compromised that understanding between us and didn't intend to do that now.

"Costilla knows you're watching him," I said.

She frowned. "No way."

"He said that he did. Does."

"Why'd he tell you that?"

"Because I asked him if he killed Kate," I said. "He said he didn't, that he was using her to feed information to you guys."

Liz squinted at me. "Maybe he said that because he didn't want to admit to her murder."

I laughed. "I was patted down twice. They knew I wasn't wired and had no weapon. He could've killed me if he wanted to. He wasn't lying to me, Liz. No reason to."

"Guy like that doesn't need a reason to lie. It's what he does."

"Okay. Did anything that you heard via Kate pan out? Meetings, deals, locations?"

Her eyes fluttered, and she looked away. I knew she was running the possibilities through her head.

"He told me the truth," I said. "I'd bet everything I have on it."

She leaned her elbows on the table. "Maybe. What else?"

I told her about how I was picked up in TJ and tried

to describe where we'd met, and about Costilla's missing money.

She tapped her index finger on the table. "She took that money, he killed her."

"I don't think so," I said. "Costilla planned on killing her. But someone else got to her first. Which leaves us with two questions. Why did she take the money, and who killed her?"

"Another deal on the side that went bad," Liz suggested.

"Could be," I said. "I feel like I'm chasing a person I never met."

She smiled briefly. "In a way, you hadn't met her. She wasn't the Kate we knew in high school."

"Not even close, apparently. Can I ask a question?"

"Might not answer it."

"Why was she inside, Liz?" I asked, looking for what seemed like one of the biggest missing pieces. "I'm just not seeing it."

She leaned back and folded her arms across her chest. I knew she was trying to decide whether she could trust me. I stayed quiet and hoped that what I'd told her so far had counted for something.

"She fit," she said finally. "She was a big-time user, Noah. She may not have looked like it, but she was. She knew the lingo, she knew what to look for, and she knew how to get close to the big guns. And she came to us."

"Isn't that unusual, though? Put a civilian in a spot like that, even with her history?"

She folded her hands on the table. "Maybe. But the DA knew about our operation, knew that she needed a deal, and knew that if it worked, he'd get some credit for brokering it."

"So it wasn't just for her to get off with probation, then?" I said. "It was political, too."

She spread her hands out in front of her. "Isn't everything?"

I shook my head, angry. "I guess."

"Noah, still. She put herself in the situation," Liz said, leaning across the table. "You carry that much heroin, you're asking for trouble. She wasn't innocent."

I considered telling her about my conversation with Ken Crier, then thought better of it. I knew the cop in Liz would be skeptical that Kate would've taken the blame for her husband.

"She didn't deserve to die, though," I said.

"No," Liz agreed. "She didn't." She reached into the breast pocket of her blouse, produced a small strip of paper, and slid it across the table to me.

"What's this?" The strip was wrinkled and torn at the corners. I unfolded it. CHARLOTTE T. was written on it.

She shook her head. "I don't know. Thought maybe you could figure it out. It was in the car with Kate's body, wadded up in the backseat. Scratch paper, most likely. Thought it was just trash at first." She paused. "Maybe it is, maybe it isn't."

I stared at it and tried to decide if it was Kate's handwriting. I had no way of knowing.

Liz leaned across the table again. "The only way her

murder is going to be solved is if you keep poking around. Everyone here and at DEA wants it quiet. They're content to blame it on Costilla."

I looked at her. "You don't think he did it then?"

"I didn't say that. I'm just saying, if someone else did do it, it won't be anyone around here that figures it out. I still think Costilla probably did it. It makes sense, no matter what he told you."

"I don't think so, Liz."

She stood and walked toward the door. "Then prove it."

 *41*

I found the Blazer out front, courtesy of Liz having it towed. I headed straight for the hospital to see Carter.

It surprised me that Liz had shared as much with me as she had. She took her work seriously and, most of the time, didn't take me too seriously. Telling me about the politics involved and handing me that scrap of paper weren't things that she normally did. It felt like we'd cleared a small hurdle in our relationship.

I took my time moving up the highway toward UCSD, staring aimlessly at the lights on Fiesta Island and Mission Bay as I moved by. I wanted nothing more than to take the exit at Grand, head straight west toward the water, grab my board, and hide from all of the crap that had entered my life by riding the water until my body went numb.

But I knew that I couldn't, so I passed the exit at Grand and tried not to think about it.

Carter's eyes widened when I walked into his room.

"Did you fall out of a building?" he asked.

"Sort of," I said, pulling what I'd started thinking of as my own personal chair next to the bed.

"What the hell happened?"

I sat down in the chair and told him about my visit with Costilla.

"You said you wouldn't do that without me," he said when I finished.

"I forgot," I said. "How are you?"

"I'm fine. Surgery was fine. I'm ready to go." He looked at me. "Jesus, I look better than you."

I rubbed my bruised cheek. "Thanks."

"Listen to me next time."

"When are you out of here?"

He dropped his head back on the pillow and heaved a pissed off, exasperated sigh. "Two days is what the doc said. I'm gonna push him on it, though."

"Don't," I said. "They know better than you do when you're ready to go home." I pulled the paper Liz had given me out of my pocket. "Here's something to keep you occupied." I handed it to him.

He let it rest in his palm. "I get shot and this is what you bring me?"

"Shut up. Liz gave it to me."

He raised an eyebrow, surprised. "The Ice Queen gave you something other than the finger?"

"We made peace."

He looked back at the paper. " 'Charlotte.' The city?"

"What about the T?"

"I don't know. Where'd Liz get it?"

"The car they found Kate in."

"The 'T' could be an initial," he said, running his finger over the paper, trying to smooth it out.

"A last name," I said. "That's my guess."

"What does Liz think it is?"

I shook my head. "She's not sure. That's why she gave it to me."

He handed it back. "That doesn't sound like her."

I told him what she'd said about finding Kate's killer.

"Still," Carter said. "Doesn't sound like Liz."

"I think the guilt is working her over pretty good."

"I suppose," he said. "But a crappy piece of paper that may have been just trash isn't much."

"No," I agreed. "It's not. But at least it's something."

The door to the room opened, and an older nurse with a gray afro stuck her head in. "Visiting hours end in five minutes, gentlemen."

I waved at her, and Carter made a face.

She smiled and shut the door.

I stood up. "I'm gonna head out. I'll come see you in the morning."

"Okay. Don't knock yourself out over this, Noah," he said, a note of caution in his voice.

"What? The paper?"

"That and everything else. It's not worth getting the shit kicked out of you. Again."

"I know."

"No, you don't," he said, tugging at the blankets

that barely covered his long frame. "Otherwise you wouldn't have gone to see Costilla."

I turned toward the door.

"Even if you figure this out," Carter continued, "what's gonna happen? Ken and Marilyn are going to give you a fat check? I know you could care less about that. Kate's not gonna be able to say thank you. No matter what you find out." He paused. "It won't bring her back."

I waved at him and left.

 *42*

Carter's words stung me.

I didn't think I was doing this to make amends for Kate, but maybe I was fooling myself. The police and the government didn't want it solved. In all likelihood, even if Kate's murder was solved, it was going to be done quietly. They would prefer that Costilla did it because it gave them one more thing to hang on him. I still wasn't convinced, and I kept turning everything over in my mind until I pulled up to Emily's.

I wasn't quite sure why I'd gone to her place. I tried telling myself that it was because I wanted to ask her more about her sister and Randall and also to see if she knew anything about the piece of paper Liz had given me. But, somewhere, in the recesses of my brain, I knew it was because I needed to settle whatever had happened between us.

I parked my car in front of her garage and walked up the stairs. I was getting used to the stiffness and soreness that permeated my body. I tried to pretend it was from a really difficult workout. And if that workout had included being used as a heavy bag, maybe my body would've bought it.

I pressed the illuminated button next to her door. After a moment, I heard her muffled voice, then footsteps. The door opened, and she stuck her head out. "Noah."

"Hey."

She opened the door enough for her to step into the opening. "I didn't know you were coming over."

"I didn't either. I was just at the hospital and thought I'd come by."

She tried to smile, but it came off as more nervous. Her hair was tousled and her cheeks flushed. She blinked several times. "Oh, um, how's Carter?"

I became keenly aware that she was not inviting me in. "He's okay. Better anyway."

She almost glanced over her shoulder, then caught herself, the look on her face telling me what I had already guessed.

"Bad timing," I said.

"Uh, yeah," she said, laughing quickly. "You could say that." She paused. "I'm sorry."

I held up my hand. "Nothing to be sorry about. I should've called."

"No," she said. "It's just . . . I don't know. I'm not getting this out."

"You don't have to," I said, backing up. "I'm on my way."

She opened the door wider. I could see she was wearing a man's dress shirt over a pair of khaki shorts. She must've noticed me looking at her clothes because she looked at herself and blushed.

"Noah," she said, then stopped. "It's my ex. The almost husband."

"Em, you don't owe me an explanation," I said, feeling the warmth in my cheeks now.

She started to say something, then looked harder at me. "What happened to your face?"

I waved a hand. "Nothing. I'll tell you later."

She looked like she wanted to say something else, then stopped. "Okay. I'll call you."

I hustled down the stairs and waved at her over my shoulder so she couldn't see the rising tide of embarrassment on my face.

 **43**

I managed not to squeal the tires of the Blazer as I left Emily's condo, but when I turned out onto Camino Del Mar, I floored it.

It wasn't that I felt that Emily and I had established some sort of relationship. We hadn't. I had avoided any discussion of a relationship on purpose, and our guilt had prevented us from doing anything else.

Seeing her, flustered and embarrassed, had rattled me, but not in the way that I would've predicted. I wasn't upset or jealous, which is what I would've expected. Instead, I was relieved. Emily and I didn't belong together, and our awkward meeting had confirmed that. Maybe I'd been trying to replace Kate with her, which was screwed up on so many levels that I didn't even want to think about it. She didn't deserve that.

And as I sped through the dark curves on Torrey Pines Road and down into La Jolla Shores, something that had been riding around in my head started to get a whole lot clearer.

I stopped at a bar in PB, already packed with an early-evening crowd, and downed a beer and a shot of tequila in about fifteen minutes. I stood at the bar, listening to Tristan Prettyman's soft voice coming from the speakers in the wall, contemplating doing something that I couldn't believe I was even giving serious thought to. I didn't want to go home and be alone. I felt like I'd been on my own all day. Before I could talk myself out of it, I left the bar and drove south.

Coronado is a small island west of the downtown area, dominated by the Naval Station and the expensive beachfront hotels, most notably the red-roofed Hotel del Coronado. Most of the families that live on Coronado have been there for years, and just about everyone seems to know each other, giving the island a feeling of having never left the fifties. The streets are narrow, the lawns are immaculate, and the view from any location—house, hotel, or restaurant—is phenomenal.

When I turned off the big blue Coronado Bridge, I dropped the windows in the SUV and let the cool evening breeze sweep across the bay into the car. My mood lightened as the island's tree-lined streets enveloped me. The hurried pace and congestion of the downtown area felt miles away, even though I could see the lights sparkling on the skyscrapers across the water.

The street I was looking for curved back with the body of the bay, and I pulled up at the curb across from the last house on the block, the bay waters lapping quietly at the retaining wall just a few feet away from me. I shut the engine off.

Many of the homes reminded me of brownstones on the East Coast, just not as tall. Straight up and down, rectangular, with flat roofs that served as decks. This particular home was whitewashed brick. A tiny walk split the emerald green lawn, with precisely trimmed rosebushes running along the front of the house. Four windows, two up and two down, dotted the face of the house, flower boxes underlining the two lower windows with bright pinks and yellows.

I got out of the car and tried to remember the last time I'd been here. It didn't come to me as I walked across the street and up the front walk into the glare of the porch light.

The front door was shut behind a slim screen door, and before I could think about it, I knocked.

No answer.

I knocked again, but I heard only silence in return.

I walked backward down the stone walk, looking up at the roof.

"You up there?" I yelled. "It's me, Noah."

I heard the scraping of an aluminum chair and hollow footsteps.

Liz looked over the edge at me. "I'm here. What's going on?"

I could see her only from the waist up, the edge of the brick rising a few feet higher than the roof. She was wearing a navy jogging tank.

"Nothing," I said.

She pulled the dark hair away from her face. "I take it you wanna come up."

I shoved my hands in my pockets. "I guess. But if you're busy . . ."

She stared at me for a minute, clearly wondering what I was doing on her front lawn.

"I'm not talking business," she said, holding a beer up in her hand. "I've had enough for today."

"Fine with me," I said.

"Door's unlocked," she said, disappearing from the edge.

So I went in.

 **44**

She was stretched out on an old chaise lounge. White shorts with a Nike swoosh matched the jogging tank. Her dark hair was flying in several different directions. Her feet were bare, running shoes and socks in a pile next to her. Two empty beer bottles stood below the armrest of the chair.

She pointed to the tiny fridge on the corner of the deck. "Beer's in there."

Four chairs dotted the deck, and a small office refrigerator sat in the corner, next to a tiny wooden table. The barbecue sat in the other corner. With no other houses to get in the way, the view of the bay and the downtown landscape was striking.

I grabbed a Dos Equis out of the fridge. "Thanks."

"I don't want to be rude," she said, looking at me. "But what the hell are you doing here?"

I sat down on the upraised brick wall that jutted

above the deck, my back to the bridge and the South Bay. "I honestly don't know."

Liz studied me for a moment, then shrugged. "Okay."

We sat there in silence, drinking our beers. I felt awkward and out of place. When we had dated, we'd spent a lot of nights on the roof, drinking, eating, and talking. Arguing a lot, too. Our relationship had moved back and forth between easy affection and irritation.

"You go see Carter again?" she asked, sitting up in the chair.

I nodded. "Yeah. He's better."

"Take a lot more than a couple of bullets to kill that elephant," she said.

"I think of him as more of a giraffe."

"Rhino fits, too."

"Yeah, it does."

We both laughed. She set her bottle down and pointed at the fridge. I reached in, grabbed a full one, opened it, and handed it to her. She took a long drink.

"Still running, I see," I said, the silence digging into me.

"About five miles every night," she said. "If I'm not worn out."

"Which you probably are more often than not."

She pursed her lips and tried to look indifferent.

"Wellton said some nice things about you today," I told her.

Her lips curled into a small smile. "John's a good guy."

"Said you take a lot of shit for partnering with him."

"I do. But screw them, you know? He's a good guy and a good cop. He probably takes shit for having a woman as a partner."

"Yeah, I guess."

We drank our beers and watched the lights shimmer on the harbor.

"Being around you again is weird," she said.

"How's that?"

She tilted her head. "Well, when things ended, it was kind of bad between us."

Our breakup had occurred outside a restaurant with each of us screaming at the other. I couldn't recall what that specific argument had been about, but the force of our words left no doubt about the finality of it all.

"Just kind of?" I said.

"Okay. Really bad. And then, with all this," she waved her hand in the air, "you've pretty much been the irritation equivalent of, say, a nail in my eardrum."

"It says a lot about you that a nail in your eardrum would be only an irritation, rather than excruciatingly painful."

She smiled. "I'm tough." She pointed the beer bottle in my direction. "But, now, I've gotta admit . . ." Her voice trailed off.

"Admit what?"

She clutched the bottle in both of her hands. "I've gotta admit I don't hate that you're here." She looked at me for a moment, then drained the beer, setting the empty bottle down next to the others. "But maybe I'm drunk."

"I'm not sure how to take that," I told her.

She swung her legs over the chair, sitting on the edge of it. "Well, neither am I." She looked at me. "Why are you here, Noah?"

I rolled my empty beer bottle between my hands. A horn blew out on the harbor from a distance, echoing softly across the water. The thought in my head that had rattled around as I left Emily's was this: if Liz had answered the door in another man's shirt, I would've been jealous and upset. I couldn't explain why, but I knew it as surely as I knew anything at that moment.

"I didn't want to be alone and I kept thinking of you," I told her. "Carter's in the hospital. Who the hell else do I hang out with?"

"Ernie?"

I grunted. "Not anymore. I put him in a bad spot and I feel like shit for doing it."

"He'll forgive you," she said.

"Maybe, but it'll be a while."

"Probably, but he will. Everyone does."

I looked at her. "Everyone does what?"

She shook her head, a faint smile on her lips. "Forgive you, Noah. Everyone does—eventually. You screw up, you do dumbass things, but in the end, you get it right. You just have to do some stupid things before you get to the right things." She paused, her blue eyes staring me down in the shadows. "It's just your way."

I gazed back at her, wondering if she realized that might have been the kindest thing she had ever said about me.

"You are drunk," I said.

She stood. "A little." She walked over to me and held out her hand. "Come on."

I grabbed her hand and pulled myself up, stifling a groan as my ribs protested that I should remain seated. "Where are we going?"

"Inside," she said, taking me with her.

"Why?" I asked, even though I had a pretty good idea.

She didn't look back. "Because I don't feel like being alone, either."

 **45**

I felt the early-morning sunlight on my face and woke up, squinting at the beam pouring into the room through a sheer curtain.

I turned over to find Liz awake, looking at me. "Hey."

She had her hands tucked between her cheek and the pillow, her hair spilling around her shoulders. "Hey."

I twisted the rest of my body around to face her and grimaced, my ribs and back knotting up in pain.

"A little sore?" she asked.

"Try a lot."

"Carter took four bullets. He makes you look like a sissy."

"I am a sissy."

She laughed. "You said it, not me."

"Actually, you did say it."

"Whatever," she said, rolling her eyes, a loopy grin

on her face. Then her smile faded. "Remember how last night I said it was weird being around you again?"

"Yeah."

"This is even weirder."

I nodded, agreeing with her.

"I didn't come here to . . . for this," I said.

"I know," she said. "If I thought you had, I would've kicked your ass off the roof."

"No doubt."

She rolled over onto her back and sighed. "But this is weird."

She had the sheet pulled up over her chest and tucked under her arms. Her shoulders were tan, probably from the running.

"So now what?" I asked.

"Little picture or big picture?" she asked, staring up at the ceiling.

"Your choice."

She turned her head to me. "I choose little picture because I have no desire to draw the big picture."

"Fine with me."

"And little picture says, what's for breakfast?"

"Am I invited to stay?"

She reached over and placed her hand lightly on my chest. "Those are hideous."

I peered down at the dark purple bruises that decorated my upper body. "Wish I could disagree." I put my hand over hers. "Gonna answer my question?"

Her eyes lingered on the bruises for a moment before she looked up at me. "Since you're already here, you can stay. But since you're the guest, you get to do the cooking." She gave a tiny grin, slid out from under the sheet, and stood. "I'm going to shower. The food better be ready by the time I'm out."

I watched her walk to the bathroom, and despite not wanting to, I smiled.

I got up, found my shorts and shirt, and headed to the kitchen. It was small but sunny, the light from the west not nearly as blinding as it had seemed in her bedroom. I found the skillet where I remembered it to be, some eggs, cheese, and mushrooms in the fridge, and threw together two omelets.

I was sliding them onto plates when she came out.

"Wow," she said, her dark hair still damp. She wore a pair of black cotton shorts and a gray T-shirt with UCSD written across it. "You were fast."

I pointed to the coffeepot. "Even got that going."

She grabbed a mug out of the cabinet. "You still averse to caffeine in the morning?"

"Yep."

"Your loss." She poured a cup from the pot, and we sat down at the table in the corner of the kitchen.

We ate in silence. Most of the time, when I'm quiet at a meal, it's because I'm uncomfortable. With Liz, it felt normal and right.

She pushed the plate away from her when she'd finished. "So. What's your plan of attack today?"

I wiped my mouth and set the fork down on my empty plate. "Got a couple of ideas."

"Like?"

"Like working on that Charlotte thing you gave me."

"I didn't give you anything," she said, looking at me over her coffee cup.

"Right. Like working on this Charlotte thing I found."

"Ah."

"Yes. Tell me something. Have you guys looked at Randall much with this?"

"Kate's husband?" she asked. She gestured with the coffee mug. "Sure. Doesn't seem to be anything there, though. He wasn't in San Diego when she died."

"Doesn't mean he couldn't have been involved, though."

"No. Why?"

"He was a user, too."

She nodded. "I know. We ran his record. He's on probation." She looked at me, puzzled. "Why would that make him wanna kill his wife?"

My thoughts flashed on my conversation with Ken again, but I pushed them aside. I didn't want to put the idea that Kate had covered for Randall out there until I thought I could get Liz to take it seriously.

"Isn't there some statistic about husbands being the most likely suspects in the deaths of their wives?" I said.

"Sure. I don't know what it is, but it's high. But you've usually got motive and some sort of evidence." She shook her head. "Randall's run clean so far."

I tried a different track. "Emily thought he was having an affair."

"Emily?"

I hesitated, feeling like she was asking me something different than what she'd intended.

"Yeah. Saw her at the funeral. She told me that he was screwing around," I said.

"Wellton interviewed her, and I know it came up then, too." Liz spun the mug on the table with her pinky finger. "But his alibi's tight. Hospital verified him being there for the last week. No way he was here."

"Just doesn't feel right, that's all," I said.

She looked at the clock on the wall and stood, grabbing the plates. "I've got to get moving. I'll look around some more, Noah, but I'm still not sure how he's connected to Kate's death. He may be an asshole, but that doesn't make him a killer."

"Yeah, you're right," I said as I pushed away from the table and slowly coaxed myself upright.

She dropped the dishes in the sink and walked over to me.

"Of course I am," she said. "I'm a homicide detective."

I smiled. "Yeah, you are."

She poked me in the chest. "I'm not gonna let this get awkward. I have no idea what this is right now."

"Me and you?"

"Yeah, me and you," she said. "And to be honest, I don't want to think about it. So, no good-bye kisses, no googly eyes, none of that crap."

"Googly eyes?" I asked.

"Yes, most likely from you," she said, trying to keep a smile from hitting her mouth. "So here it is. I'm glad you came by last night and I'm glad you're here this morning. But let's just see what happens. No promises. Alright?"

"No," I said.

She looked surprised. "No?"

"I'm kissing you good-bye," I said as I leaned over.

When I pulled away, she kept her eyes closed for an extra moment before opening them. "Alright, good decision. Yeah. But definitely no googly eyes."

 **46**

As I put the key in the ignition of the Blazer, it occurred to me that I hadn't mentioned to Liz anything about the key Emily had given me. I still wasn't sure if it would tell me anything and Liz had been skeptical of my other ideas, so I didn't see the point of bringing it up. But I made a mental note to ask Carter about the key the next time I visited the hospital.

I drove back to my place and rather than shower right away, grabbed my board and headed out to the small swells that were rising along the shoreline. The water felt good on my body and eased the soreness.

As I cut through the water, I managed not to think about Kate or Randall or Costilla. The great thing about surfing is that you can lose yourself in it. Whether you're smashing into the lip or gazing into the front end of a tight barrel, everything else in the world falls away. Concentrate on your footwork, feel that back anchor foot driving the board back and forth, and let the rails slice through the face of the water and take you somewhere you've never been before.

In between sets, sitting on my board, watching the morning walkers along the shore, I did think about Liz, though. The night had felt like some sort of breakthrough. I didn't know exactly what it was we were breaking through, but I definitely felt good about it. I hadn't thought about Emily, and that fact made me realize that what she and I had been doing together was probably more out of confusion than anything else. What I didn't feel good about was having to have that conversation with Emily.

I watched a small set roll by and below me and continued floating in the water.

Regardless of whom Emily and I had been with, the conversation would be uneasy. It always is. Even if we both recognized that we had gotten together for the wrong reasons, our relationship would probably be tense and awkward in whatever shape it remained.

A nice three footer curled up behind me. I moved to my stomach, paddled in front of it, and let it pick me up. I pushed up to a crouch and dropped into the small face, a tiny ripple of excitement working through my stomach as the board slid to the bottom of the wave. It closed out quickly, and I bobbed my way to the shore, the white water sending me in.

After showering and tossing on a T-shirt and a pair of shorts, I took the cordless phone out onto the patio with a phone book and a notepad, along with the scrap of paper Liz had given me. I paged through the phone

book, without really thinking I'd find something.
Looking for Charlotte T. would have to start somewhere, no matter how tedious and silly it seemed.

After thirty minutes of looking, I'd located only a
Charlotte Thompson in El Cajon and a Charlotte Terry
in Mira Mesa. Both were on the other side of sixty, and
neither knew Kate or Randall Crier.

I called directory assistance in Marin County and
the not-so-friendly operator told me that she had over
twenty Charlottes with the last initial T and that she
could not give them to me over the phone. She informed me that I could find current phone books at my
local library and hung up.

I sat there for a few minutes watching the people
strolling on the boardwalk. The sun was high, but haze
from the morning marine layer was muting its glare.
The people who had slept in late were just now arriving
at the beach, toting chairs, coolers, and kids, and finding a spot in the sand to spend the next couple of hours.

I called directory assistance in Marin again, got a
different operator, and asked for the number to Randall's hospital.

"St. Andrew's," a pleasant voice said. "How can I direct your call?"

"Not sure," I said, scrambling. "I'm looking for a
Charlotte, but I don't know her last name."

"Do you know the department, sir?"

"I don't, I'm sorry. My answering machine ate most
of the message and I have no idea what the call is re-
garding."

"That's alright," she said. "Happens to the best of us. Let me check . . . okay. I have two Charlottes in the directory. Dr. Charlotte Kollack in oncology and Charlotte Truman, our deputy administrator."

Bingo. "Let's try the latter. I think I might've heard Truman on the machine."

"I'll connect you to that office," she said. "One moment."

Ten seconds later, a voice came on the line. "Charlotte Truman's office."

"Is Ms. Truman in?" I asked.

"No, I'm afraid not," the female voice said. "She's out for the week."

"The whole week?"

"Yes, sir. She's down in Los Angeles for the conference at the Bonaventure and won't be back until next Monday."

"I see."

"Can I take a message, sir?" she asked. "She's checking in periodically."

I thought about it and decided against it. I told her no thanks and hung up.

I figured a drive up to LA would get me a quicker answer.

 **47**

One of the things I admired about San Diego was that despite the fact that the population in the county continued to grow, it hadn't changed its attitude. Sure, there were more cars on the road and housing prices were soaring, but no one seemed stressed out by it. Everyone was happy to be in a beautiful city by the ocean with weather that bordered on spectacular.

I couldn't say the same for Los Angeles. The Angelenos had seemed to adopt a hustle and bustle lifestyle that was more appropriate for the East Coast. The result was something that gave the city the feeling of a spoiled younger sibling, and I rarely enjoyed venturing into the area.

The drive up the snarled 5 and 405 through Orange County and Long Beach took me a little over two hours. I read somewhere that Southern California possessed eleven miles of permanently clogged freeway where the traffic was at a constant standstill. As I took the interchange to the 110 and entered the massive maze of concrete and asphalt that made up downtown Los Angeles, I thought eleven miles might have been a conservative guess.

The Westin Bonaventure is LA's largest convention hotel, a series of circular glass towers that rise out of the financial district like something from the future. It boasted of spectacular views of downtown Los Angeles from the higher floors, but never mentioned the possibility of those views being choked off by the smog.

I parked in the massive garage and found my way inside the hotel. The enormous six-story atrium, housing restaurants, bars, and shops, gave me the feel that I was in an oversized greenhouse. I saw a sign that directed me toward the conference and meeting rooms and found a tall thin man in his forties sitting at a table next to a giant easel that said CALIFORNIA PHYSICIANS AND ADMINISTRATORS ASSOCIATION CONFERENCE.

"What can I help you find?" he asked, smiling.

"Well, I'm not sure," I said. "I'm actually looking for a person, but I have no idea where she might be."

"Presenter or attendee?" he asked, grabbing a thick black binder from the corner of the table.

"Don't know that either," I said, shrugging.

He clutched the binder and looked at me. "Sir, are you here for the conference?"

"Actually, no," I said, shoving my hands in my pockets. "I'm trying to track down a friend."

"A friend?"

"Her office told me I could find her here," I said, trying to look harmless. "Charlotte Truman?"

He set the book on the table, frown lines wrinkling his forehead. "You're a friend?"

Can't fool everybody all of the time. I reached into my back pocket and flipped my license open at him. "Not really, but I do need to find Ms. Truman."

He stared at the license, the lines on his forehead deepening. "Is she in trouble? Has something happened?"

"No, everything's fine. I just need to talk to her." I smiled. "I'm not looking to rock the boat."

He looked at the license again, then at me. "I hope not. She's giving the keynote address this evening. It would be a disaster if she weren't able to do that."

I tried to look sympathetic to his cause. "I promise. My visit will do nothing to change her availability for this evening."

He bit his bottom lip for a moment, clearly not wanting to be a party to the potential ruin of the conference.

"Look, you told me she's speaking tonight," I said. "If you won't tell me where she is now, I'll have no choice but to hang around until I find her tonight." I shoved my wallet back into my shorts. "Your call."

His left eye twitched, then he opened the binder. He flipped through several pages, ran a bony finger down one, and tapped the middle of the page.

"The Santa Anita Room," he said, pointing to his right. "Last room at the end of this hall."

"I appreciate it," I told him and started in that direction.

"Sir?"

I turned back to him.

He held up a plastic badge with a nylon string attached to it. The card in the clear plastic badge said VISITOR.

"This might make it easier," he said, offering it to me. "You'll look like you're supposed to be here."

I took the badge and hung it around my neck. "That, buddy, is something I don't hear too often."

 *48*

The Santa Anita Room was one of those sterile spaces that could be divided up into sections with ugly partitions, but currently it was wide open and completely filled for whatever was going on.

About seventy-five tables dotted the room, six chairs around each. I didn't see an empty seat anywhere.

The attendees were focused on a long table toward the front, where four people sat. Three men and a woman. The woman was attractive. Early forties, auburn hair cut to her shoulders, an expensive-looking navy suit. She gestured with her hands as she spoke.

"Our job," she said, friendly but confident, "is to deal with the people, and the issues, that the rest of the hospital won't. Can't, in fact. They aren't equipped with the knowledge to make those kinds of decisions. Their job is to save the patients. Ours is to ensure that they can continue to do that."

A round of applause arose from the tables and one of the men on the panel stood.

"I think we'll end on that note," he said, smiling broadly at the audience, then at the three people to his left. "Let's thank our panelists today. Chandler Mott, Damian Taitano, and Charlotte Truman."

I eased into the back corner of the room as the audience stood and again applauded. The people began to trickle out of the room, smiling and whispering to one another, apparently having learned some big secret to hospital administration.

I let the room nearly clear out before moving toward the front and Charlotte Truman.

"That was fabulous," a woman was gushing at her. "Exactly what most of us needed to hear."

Charlotte Truman nodded graciously. "Thank you. That's kind of you to say."

"I mean," the woman continued, "I don't think my hospital has any idea of the confrontations that I face on a daily basis."

Truman began gathering up her belongings. "No, they probably don't. But that doesn't mean you're any less valuable. Part of your job is to be good at thankless endeavors."

"Yes, yes, I guess it is," the woman said, nodding vigorously, as if the thought had never occurred to her.

Truman picked up the last of her folders and looked at the woman. "Great to meet you."

"Oh, no," the woman said. "The pleasure was mine."

The woman turned from Truman and pounced on the man that had been sitting next to her.

I caught up to Charlotte Truman in the middle of the room.

"Quite a presentation," I said, falling in step next to her.

She gave me what I thought to be a very practiced smile. "Thank you. You really think so?"

"Actually, I didn't hear a word of it," I said. "I was just going by her reaction."

She cocked her head in my direction, large green eyes sparkling. "It actually sucked."

"You fooled her?"

"Fooling them is the key to getting invited to these things," she said. "Anything is better than working, right?"

We walked out into the hallway.

"I suppose," I said.

She stopped. "You don't look like an attendee."

"Why's that?"

"The visitor badge for starters." She looked me up and down. "And most of these people don't own shorts and T-shirts. I imagine they sleep in their suits."

"Makes it tough to relax," I said.

"Yes, it does. What can I do for you?"

"Maybe nothing," I said. "I'm taking a chance."

"Shorts, T-shirt, and a risk taker. Definitely not a hospital administrator," she said with an amused smile.

"I'm an investigator," I said.

She raised an eyebrow, suddenly wary. "If you're insurance, I'm not talking to you outside my office."

I shook my head. "No. Something else. A doctor at your hospital."

Her eyebrow fell. "I'm not sure I'm following, Mr. . . ."

"Braddock," I said. "But call me Noah."

"Well, Noah, what is it that you're here for?"

"I'm doing a background check on a doctor who works at St. Andrew's. Dr. Randall Tower."

Until that moment, she'd seemed unflappable. Completely comfortable in her skin and her surroundings, totally in command of the room and the subject about which she was speaking.

Randall's name destroyed all that.

The color drained from her face. "What the hell is this?"

"You know him?"

She shifted the folders in her arms. "He works at the hospital. Of course I know him."

"Friends outside the hospital?"

Her eyes narrowed, the easygoing demeanor vanished. "What are you doing?"

"I'm not sure. What am I doing?"

"Pissing me off, for one," she said, the color rising back to her cheeks.

I decided to be straight. "I'm looking into his wife's death. Her body was found in the trunk of her car along with this piece of paper." I pulled the scrap from my pocket and handed it to her.

"Kate's dead?" she asked.

"Yes."

She blinked rapidly for a moment, then stared at the piece of paper. She shook her head. "So she knew."

"Excuse me?"

Charlotte handed me the paper back. "Look, you found this and you found me. My guess is you know more than you're letting on, seeing if I'll spill the beans for you." She smiled but it wasn't warm. "Randall and I were sleeping together, but I think you already knew that."

"I had an idea." I looked at her. "Can we talk for a few minutes?"

She paused for a moment. Then, "Kate's really dead? You're not kidding me, right?"

"No, Ms. Truman," I told her. "Kate Crier is dead."

She winced slightly, the word "dead" making an impression. She started walking again.

"I can talk for a few minutes. But only a few minutes," she said. "Because talking about him for any longer than that will make me ill."

 *49*

We walked outside onto the expansive pool deck. I bought a cup of coffee and a soda from a pushcart under a big palm tree. Charlotte was sitting on the edge of the stone retaining wall that ringed a small garden in the middle of the courtyard. I handed her the coffee and sat next to her.

She squinted into the afternoon sunlight. "You from LA?"

"No, San Diego."

"And you came up here to see me?"

I nodded.

She sipped from the paper cup. "Well, I guess I should talk to you then."

"I'd appreciate it."

"I'll bet," she said, setting the coffee next to her. "I met Randall last year. I knew his name as an employee before that, maybe said hello to him a time or two, but didn't really get to know him until last year."

We watched a group spill out from the hotel, deep in conversation.

"He had to come see me about some problems he was having," she said.

"Drugs?"

She glanced in my direction. "You've done your homework," she said, then after a pause, continued. "The hospital put him on probation because of his drug problem. It's my job to deal with that kind of thing. Not always fun, but it's my job."

"Why wasn't he fired?" I asked. "Seems like a huge risk keeping a drug-addict doctor on staff."

She crossed her legs and picked up her cup. "You'd be surprised. A good portion of my job is working with our employees who have what I'll call issues." She sipped the coffee. "Alcohol, drugs, marital problems, financial problems. Doctors have it all. They aren't immune from our cultural pitfalls. I could tell you that they are more susceptible, but that's just my opinion."

"The result of a high-pressure profession?"

"Sure. They get sucked in like the rest of us." She rolled the coffee cup slowly between her hands. "Anyway, it was his first offense, as it were. He was receiving counseling and we kept him away from patients for a while to make sure he didn't slip up."

"What was he doing if he wasn't seeing patients?"

She smiled at me. "Fucking me, mostly."

I took a drink of my soda and said nothing.

"I was immediately attracted to him," she said,

brushing an auburn curl off her forehead. "I knew he was married and thought a bit of harmless flirting would be just that. Harmless." She clucked her tongue against the roof of her mouth. "I'd just gone through an ugly divorce and was not in the right place. He told me the drug counseling was tough on him, that his wife didn't understand what he was going through."

I took another drink of the soda and resisted the urge to point out Randall's obvious lie. If anyone would've known what he was going through, it would've been Kate.

"He didn't have a lot to do without patients to see," Charlotte continued. "Some paperwork, but not much else. He came to my office frequently." She paused, pursing her lips. "One thing led to another."

"Were you in love with him?" I asked.

"Thought I was," she answered. "He's handsome, charming, intelligent. Gave me back what I'd lost in my divorce. But I started to realize that wasn't what he was looking for."

"So did you break it off?"

She finished the coffee, then shook her head. "Not right away. I was enjoying having someone around. I stayed with it until about a month ago." She paused and set the now empty cup on the ledge. "I realized I wasn't the only one."

"You mean Kate."

She turned to me. "No. I had somehow rationalized having an affair with a married man. Got it in my head that I was the good one, Kate was the bad one. I was the one he needed, not his unsympathetic wife."

I frowned. "I don't understand then."

"He was seeing someone besides me and besides his wife," she said, sadness in her eyes. "His cell phone was ringing with calls he wouldn't take in front of me, I was getting hang-ups on my home line. He started making excuses to get out of meeting me. So I asked him."

"And he didn't deny it?"

"No," she said, almost laughing. "Can you believe that? I don't know if he thought I wouldn't care or maybe he just didn't care. I don't know. I think he was surprised when I said that I was done with the whole thing. But I don't think he was sad." She looked at me again. "I could rationalize being the other woman to his wife, but I couldn't justify being one of the other women. Stupid, but I guess I have my limits."

"Any idea if Kate knew about the affairs?"

"No," Charlotte said, shaking her head. "I didn't think she did. That's why I was so surprised when you showed me that piece of paper."

"Did you know Kate?"

"Not really. Saw her at a hospital function once or twice." She smiled ruefully. "Not a great idea to make friends with the wife of your lover, you know?"

"I suppose," I said.

She looked at her watch and stood. "I've gotta get back in there. Time to wow them again."

"I'm gonna need to tell the police working Kate's investigation about you," I told her. "They'll want to talk to you."

"That's fine," she said. "I really am sorry. You shocked the hell out of me when you said she was dead. I don't feel good about that."

I nodded and stood. "One more question, Charlotte. Any idea who the other woman was?"

"None," she said, straightening the folders under her arm. "And that was probably for the best."

"Why's that?"

She brushed the hair from her forehead with her free hand. "Because I would've done one of two things. One, I would've found her and kicked her ass. I was furious when he admitted it and I would've confronted her if I could have." She smiled, but it didn't seem happy. "Or, two, I would've told Kate about her. Just to hurt everybody." She paused, staring at me. "You ever cheated on anybody, Noah?"

I thought about it and didn't know how to answer, so I just shrugged.

"Then you haven't," she said. "Because the second you get involved in it, the second you can call yourself an adulterer, you change. You know you're different than you were before," she said, shaking her head like she wanted to remove the memory from her mind. "And, trust me, it's not for the better."

I watched Charlotte Truman walk back into the hotel, taking her guilt with her.

 **50**

The late-afternoon sun burned brightly as I drove back to San Diego. The traffic choked up in the hills of Mission Viejo, and the half-moon-shaped Dana Harbor looked like a bathtub out in the distance, filled with tiny sailboats as I crawled along the winding concrete highway.

I called Liz at the office, but got her voice mail. I told her about Charlotte, explained why she might want to talk to her, and gave my opinion that she probably didn't have anything to do with Kate's death. I knew Liz would interview her anyway, looking for something I might have missed. I thought about asking Liz to call me, but instead said, "See ya later."

I turned Jack Johnson up on the radio, traffic lightening as I passed through San Clemente. I glanced wistfully at the crowded waters at Trestles, which offered arguably some of the most maneuverable waves in southern California. I didn't have my board or the time, but that didn't prevent me from momentarily wishing that I could stop for a quick session. Instead, I continued driving and let Johnson's guitar and smooth vocals wash some of the tension out of my body as I thought about my conversation with Charlotte Truman.

I believed the things she had told me. I could understand how Randall must've seemed attractive. Her telling of the story laid most of the blame in her lap, but I knew that Randall was an equal party. There are always at least two pieces to the puzzle. In this case, though, there seemed to be three, and I didn't know where I was going to find the third.

I pondered that as I walked into Carter's hospital room. He was staring at the television in the far corner of the room, the remote in his hand.

He motioned to the screen. "I am never going to a game again."

I saw several Padres players walking off the field, heads hung low, as the entire Dodgers team danced around home plate.

"Yes you will," I said.

He shook his head violently like a child disagreeing with a parent. "No way, dude. I'm finished with them."

"Then who are you gonna root for?"

"I don't know. Maybe the Devil Rays. They don't have any fans."

I sat down in my chair. "Whatever."

He clicked the TV off with the remote and dropped it in his lap. "Where you been?"

"That is a loaded question," I said, not sure where to begin.

Carter studied me for a moment, leaned over the edge of the bed. "You were with Emily again."

"No I wasn't."

"Yeah you were. I can tell."

"What?"

"You had sex."

"How can you tell that?"

He pointed to my head. "Those lines in your forehead are gone."

"That means nothing."

He leaned back in his bed. "Does too."

"I haven't seen Emily," I said.

"Well, you did something with somebody," he said, folding his arms across his chest.

We stared at each other for a minute, neither of us blinking.

His eyebrows rose up slowly, and the rest of his face broke into a look of horror. "No."

"Afraid so."

He shook his head slowly. "No. No way."

"Yup."

"The Ice Queen?"

A big grin was my only response.

He dropped his head dramatically back onto his pillow. "I'm in here for a couple of days and you start making decisions like someone stole your brain."

"I'm not here to argue about this with you," I said.

"Well, somebody's gotta argue it because being with her ain't right."

"Isn't that a country song?"

"Shut up, Noah," he said, raising his head up again. "Were you completely ripped? Or maybe in a coma?"

I showed him my middle finger, but smiled. "No."

He looked at me, then waved his hand in the air. "I don't wanna talk about this right now. My heart can't take it."

"You weren't shot in the heart."

"Whatever. Where else have you been?"

I told him about my trip to Los Angeles to see Charlotte.

He whistled when I finished. "Randall just can't seem to do the right thing."

"I know."

"But you don't think she had anything to do with Kate?"

"She's clean," I told him. "She's a pistol, for sure. But she was pretty honest about the whole deal. Didn't blame Randall for any of it."

"Maybe that's what she wanted you to think."

"I don't think so, but I left Liz a message about her anyway."

Carter winced at Liz's name. Then he shivered like he had goosebumps.

"I need to ask him about this other woman," I said. "She may be just like Charlotte, but I want to talk to her."

"Yeah, I agree," he said.

I thought about another loose end. "Do you have

that key Emily gave me?" I asked. "I gave it to you right before . . ."

". . . you got me shot," he finished. He looked over to the small dresser sitting under the television. "Top drawer. It's with my wallet and watch."

I walked over and opened the drawer. The key was resting on top of his wallet. I turned back to him.

"Charlie Stratton," he said, anticipating my question. "He has a kiosk in Clairemont Square, by the theater. Makes keys on the spot." He nodded at the key in my hand. "He'll know."

I put the key in my pocket. "Okay. You alright here tonight? You want anything?"

He shook his head. "No. I'm not feeling so good anyway."

I walked over to the bed. "Why? What's wrong?"

He leaned forward, clutching his stomach. "Oh, God."

I grabbed the blue, half-moon-shaped tray off the shelf next to his bed and slid it onto his lap.

He flopped back, waving it away. "Never mind. I guess it was just the thought of you and the Ice Queen again."

I flipped the tray at his head. "I gotta go."

He ducked. "Where?"

"See Emily."

"Jesus. Aren't we the sexual deviant?"

"No," I said, frowning, walking toward the door. "I need to set things straight."

"Noah?"

I opened the door and turned back to him. "What?"

"Last night," he said. "With Liz. Seriously. You feel good about it?"

"As good as I've felt about anything this week," I said.

He nodded solemnly, cracked a small smile in my direction, then doubled over, retching loudly.

 *51*

I pulled into Emily's condo community in Del Mar and parked in front of her stairs. I wasn't looking forward to the conversation, but I knew I needed to clear the air. The longer I let it go, the more difficult it would be for me to see her, something that was going to happen if I was going to figure out what happened to Kate.

I walked up the steps to her door and knocked. I waited a minute, then knocked again. Still no answer.

I ran back to my car, scribbled a quick note, and ran it up to her door. I knew that I was getting off easy, but I tried to convince myself that leaving a note was at least pushing the issue.

As I drove down PCH, the sun was starting to dip and I decided to pull off and walk the beach at Torrey Pines State Beach. I knew I couldn't make it to Claire-mont Square in time to talk with Carter's friend about the key, and I'd found that walking the sand at dusk does wonders to organize my thoughts.

I'd walked a couple hundred yards to the south, just to the edge of the bluffs, and was kicking myself for not having my board in the rental car when I recognized a familiar face walking in my direction.

Emily smiled at me as we met. "Hey, stranger."

"Hi. I was actually just up at your place."

"I wasn't there."

"Got that. I left a note."

She wrinkled her nose. "Sounds serious."

"Sort of," I said, a mixture of relief and dread coursing through me in anticipation of our impending conversation.

She tugged on the hem of her gray T-shirt. "Noah, last night—"

I held up my hand. "Let's not apologize or do any of that stuff. That's what I wanted to talk about."

She motioned toward the rocks at the base of the cliff, and we walked over to them and sat down.

"I didn't know he was coming over," she said before I could say anything. "I hadn't seen him in a couple of months. Things just kind of went nuts." She paused. "But I told him that last night was one night. That's it."

I nodded. "You don't have to explain anything to me, Em. Really."

"I know. But it was awkward."

"Yeah, it was." We watched the water for a minute before I spoke again. "Emily, I just don't think this is a good idea."

She looked surprised. "What? You and me?"

I nodded. "There's too much going on right now. With both of us."

She bit her bottom lip, her gaze now riveted on the surf. "Okay."

My stomach dropped further. "I don't have a clue what I'm doing, Em. I really don't. I'm trying to make Kate's death a priority and starting a relationship with you at the same time . . . it just doesn't feel right."

"Fine," she said, her voice a dull monotone.

"And we're gonna be around each other," I said before I lost the courage to keep talking about it. "I need to be able to talk to you without feeling weird around you. And if something's going on with us, I don't think that's gonna work."

"I get it," she said, but still didn't look at me.

We sat there in silence. The sun sunk further, turning the ocean from a dark blue to more of a metallic hue. The waves got smaller, long lines of foam washing easily to the shore.

"This feels like it's about last night," she said finally, hugging her knees to her chest.

"It's not," I said. "I promise. Maybe last night made it clearer to me. I don't know. But this is about you and me—nothing else."

She turned to look at me. No tears in her eyes. I'm not sure what I expected. Maybe a little anger, maybe a little sadness. But her expression was blank.

She brushed the blond hair from her face and stood. "Thanks."

"Thanks?"

"For letting me know," she said.

I stood. "Emily, I didn't—"

It was her turn to hold up her hand. "I mean it. Thanks for letting me know where I stand."

She walked past me, up the beach toward the parking lot, leaving me without anything else to say or anyone to say it to.

 **52**

I spent the night wrestling with Emily's reaction to me and new thoughts about Liz. I ended up getting about two hours of sleep. When I woke, I felt too sluggish to hit the water or take a run, so I took a long shower, read the paper, and watched a thick marine layer build over the coast. A day without sunshine.

I drove up to Clairemont about mid-morning to see Carter's key guy. About twenty minutes from the beaches, the only notable thing about the area was that the high school with the same name was rumored to have been where Cameron Crowe did his undercover research for *Fast Times at Ridgemont High*. The school did not put that on its enrollment materials.

Situated between the canyons, the area housed middle-class homes and lots of strip malls. Clairemont Square had undergone numerous renovations, trying to keep up with the changing retail times, but it never seemed to quite make it with each new face-lift. The giant theater that still loomed as the anchor of the out-door plaza was *the* place to see movies when I was a kid. Now it ran films you could see at half price if you didn't mind the grainy print quality or that it had already been out for a month.

I found the kiosk in the middle of the plaza. A guy with a long ponytail was lounging on a tall director's chair, his feet up on the cart and a cigarette in his mouth. Long, skinny arms emerged from a grubby white tank top that matched the dirty jeans and work boots.

"You Charlie?" I asked, admiring the vast quantity of keys hanging in every possible place on the cart.

He pulled the cigarette from his lips and squinted at me. "Yeah. What can I do for you, man?"

"Got a question about a key."

He spread his arms wide, grinning. "Well, you've found heaven then."

I pulled the key out of the pocket of my shorts. "Carter Hamm sent me."

He tapped the cigarette and ash fell to the ground. He cocked an eyebrow at me. "No shit? My good buddy Carter?"

"Yeah. Said you might be able to tell me what this belongs to." I handed the key to him.

He jammed the cigarette back into his lips and turned the key over in his palm a couple of times. "Probably." He grinned at me. "For the right price."

"I said Carter sent me."

He pulled the cigarette out of his mouth, tossed it to

the ground, and stepped on it. "Exactly. That's why it'll only cost you twenty instead of forty."

I extracted a twenty from my wallet and handed it to him. "What a deal."

His laugh sounded like a hiss. "I know, dude. You're lucky."

Charlie turned around, his ponytail whipping over his shoulder. His bare neck exposed a tattoo of a black panther with its fangs bared. I tried to imagine the pain of ink needles dancing around the top of my spine.

He turned back around, an old metal toolbox in his hand. He set the box on the cart and opened it up. He rummaged through what looked to be thousands of keys. Old, new, shiny, rusted, big, small.

"Heard Carter was in the hospital," Charlie said, moving some more keys around.

I tried not to look surprised. "Yeah. Actually, he is."

He hissed or laughed or whatever it was again. "That dude gets in more shit."

"He's gonna be alright."

"Good to hear." He stared at a particular key he'd pulled from the toolbox, then at my key. "That's it."

"What?"

He held up my key. "This goes to one of them rental lockers. Put a quarter in and pull the key out and it's locked, you know?"

"Yeah. Like at the airport."

He shrugged. "Or Sea World. Or wherever."

"Is it possible to tell where it came from? I mean, exactly."

Charlie held the key up and flipped it around with his fingers, then nodded. "Probably." He smiled at me.

"For a price," I said.

His grin grew. "Right on, brother. Something with a one and a couple of zeros in it."

I pulled four twenties, two tens, and one of my cards out of my wallet and handed them over. "I need to know as soon as possible."

He shoved the money in his pocket and examined my card. "An investigator. Like Magnum, dude?"

"Just like him."

"Cool," he said, nodding his approval. He folded the key in my card and slid them into the front pocket of his jeans. "I'll call you."

"When?"

He smiled. "When I know, Magnum."

I walked away wondering if I was the only normal friend that Carter had.

 **53**

I drove home, not knowing what else to do, and unexpectedly found Liz waiting in front of my door.

I waved. "Hi."

She wore faded blue jeans and a sleeveless navy blouse that buttoned up the middle. Her hair was swept over to the left side of her face, her sunglasses resting atop the mane. The thick-heeled sandals made her a couple inches taller than normal.

"Hi," she said, a reluctant smile on her face.

"Just couldn't stay away," I said, walking up to her.

"I got your message yesterday," she said, ignoring my comment. "Tell me more."

I motioned for her to follow me in to my place. We sat on the sofa, and I told her about my conversation with Charlotte Truman.

When I finished, she shook her head. "Randall is one cool guy."

"Sure—if by cool you mean an arrogant, self-important, spineless asshole."

She folded her arms across her chest and crossed her legs. "Alright, alright. I admit he's not as innocent as I originally thought, but I still think Costilla's the guy, Noah. Randall has an alibi and this Truman lady doesn't sound like much. We'll talk to her, but you said yourself she didn't seem like a suspect."

"No, I don't think Charlotte did anything other than make a poor decision," I said. "But all this crap keeps leading back to Randall."

"Alibi is airtight," she said. "He was at the hospital. We already checked it out."

"Doesn't mean he wasn't involved," I said.

"How so?"

"Could've hired someone, I don't know. But he just seems wrong."

"A lot of guys cheat on their wives. Doesn't mean they want them dead."

Her arms were lean and toned, her shoulders tan. I tried not to stare.

"I'm gonna tell you something and I just want you to listen for a second," I said. "Okay?"

"I get nervous when you say things like that to me," Liz said, shifting her weight on the sofa.

"What if I told you that Kate covered for him when she was arrested? That the heroin was his, not hers."

She looked at me like I was the one with the drug problem. "What?"

I told her what Ken and Randall told me. She listened quietly, biting her bottom lip a couple of times.

"Noah, come on," she said when I finished. "You really buy that? She was a user, a junkie. Lying is a way of life."

"Ken was convinced and Randall confirmed it. He admitted that it was his."

"Ken is her father. He's always going to place the blame elsewhere."

"How do you explain Randall then? Why tell me it was his if it wasn't?"

Liz's look was skeptical. "I don't know why he'd say it, but what does that really give us? Even if that's true, how does that give him motive to kill her? Jesus, if anything, Randall probably is living with the guilt complex to end all guilt complexes. Maybe telling you all this is a way for him to try and absolve himself."

"What if Randall was afraid she'd turn on him? Recant her story and tell everyone the drugs were his," I suggested. "Maybe going undercover and working with Costilla were harder than she imagined, and Randall saw that and started worrying that Kate couldn't hold up her end of the deal."

Liz leaned forward, tapping her fingers on her knees. "I know you're having trouble with this, Noah."

"This?" I said, annoyed that she wasn't buying into my logic.

"Yeah, this," she said, widening her eyes. "Kate was different. It wasn't the same Kate. You can't seem to grasp that, which I understand. I do. But, Noah, clean or not, she was different. You didn't know her anymore. You had no idea about her drug problem or what was going on with her marriage. And, somehow, you've got it screwed into your head that you could've saved her."

"No," I said.

"Yes," she said, nodding her head. "You think that if you'd stayed in her life, everything would have been different. And maybe it would have, but the chances that you could've prevented her from experimenting with heroin, marrying an asshole, and digging a legal hole for herself are slim. Slimmer than slim." She paused, fixing her eyes on me. "And you need to deal with that." She cleared her throat, and her look softened. "I'm sorry she's dead, but Randall didn't do it. I'm pretty confident on that."

I stood up and walked over to the patio door, mulling over what she'd said. Outside, the gray sky put a silver tint in the water and there was a noticeable lack of runners and skaters, thanks to the cloudy weather. I wasn't sure if Liz's thinking was colored by the guilt she felt at letting Kate slip through her protection. I knew she wanted to nail Costilla. She had a lot more invested in him than I did.

But she had a point. It wasn't so much that I thought I could've really saved Kate. My reasons for wanting to figure out Kate's death were more selfish than that. I wanted to save the memories I had of her before all of this occurred. For so long, she had been the only good thing in my life. I never knew my father and my mother was a relentless drunk, incapable of providing me with the one thing that I didn't know my life was missing until Kate had given it to me.

Love.

I had always associated that emotion with Kate, as she was the person who showed me how it felt to be cared about and to be loved for the first time. I didn't want that memory ripped out of my life by the things that happened when we went our separate ways.

But maybe I didn't have a choice.

"So if it's Costilla," I said, turning around to Liz, "there's really nothing to be done. Right?"

She shrugged. "Not at the moment, no. It's a matter of putting a case together against him. Her murder will be one more thing added to the potential list."

"Can you add her murder if you don't have direct evidence, though?"

She thought about it for a moment, then shook her head. "No. We'll need something."

"Which you don't have right now."

"No."

It was an ugly circle to think about.

 **54**

Liz and I decided to head over to Roberto's to grab some lunch. We sat down with my rolled tacos and her enchilada at a stone table facing the street.

"How's Carter?" she asked.

"Better," I told her. "Saw him yesterday. He's getting antsy."

She stabbed the enchilada with her plastic fork. "Big surprise there."

"He'll probably be out in another day or two."

She set her fork down and wiped her mouth with the paper napkin. "You tell him?"

"Tell him what?"

"That Elvis lives." She rolled her eyes. "About you and me."

I laughed. "Oh. I didn't know there was a you and me. Yet."

"I don't either. Yet. Just wondering if you opened your big mouth."

I finished off the first of the tacos. "He sorta guessed."

"You guys are like a couple of sorority girls," she said, shaking her head.

"A little, yeah." I bit into another of the tacos. "So, is there a you and me?"

A Harley went ripping down Mission, the engine tearing into the air. We watched it zip past us.

"Last time didn't go so well," Liz said.

"Nope."

"I'm not looking for that to happen again."

"Me either."

She finished off the enchilada and pushed the paper boat away from her. "I can't guarantee that it won't."

"Me either."

She leaned forward, her elbows on the table. "You were the last person I expected to see show up at my house the other night. In fact, if you'd asked to come over, I probably would've told you no." She touched her index finger to her lips for a moment, a gesture that I knew meant she was measuring her words. "But I'm not disappointed that you came over, I'm not disappointed that you spent the night, and I'm not disappointed that we're sitting here."

"I hate to disappoint."

"Could be complicated," she said, raising an eyebrow. "My job, your job. We've each wanted to tear the other's head off just in the last week."

"I never wanted to tear your head off," I said. "Maybe kick it once or twice."

"Exactly. Could be complicated."

"Is this your way of not giving me an answer?"

She smiled and tilted her head. "I'm a bitch. No doubt about it. You said so yourself. I'm not gonna change."

"I'm not asking you to," I said.

"Plus, I hate Carter."

I grinned. "You say you hate Carter, but you really don't."

"Most of the time, I'm pretty sure I do."

"He doesn't hate you."

She pointed at me. "If there is a me and you, that is your first official lie during the new me-and-you era."

I waved a hand in the air. "Most people have trouble with Carter. I'm better than most."

That earned an outright laugh. "If you do say so yourself."

"And I do."

We sat there looking at each other, the remnants of lunch dirtying the table between us. She may have been a pain in the ass, she may have been unreasonable, and she may have been hardheaded. She probably thought I was all those things, too. But I enjoyed being with Liz. She knew me differently than other people did, and I liked the intimacy of that. I struggled to feel comfortable with many people in the world, but with her, it happened easily. And to top it all off, she had never been unattractive. I was a sucker for blue eyes and black hair, and her blue eyes and black hair were better than most.

"Okay," she said finally.

"Okay?"

"We'll try the me and you thing." She aimed a finger in my direction. "Try not to screw it up."

"Same to you," I said.

 **55**

After lunch, Liz headed back to her office. She said she would check on Charlotte Truman and see if anything popped up. I didn't think that it would, but I felt better that the investigation would be thorough.

I decided to drive up to La Jolla to the Criers' home. When I arrived, Ken and Marilyn were sitting on the stone steps that led to their front door. Ken wore his usual sharply creased khakis with a bright-red golf shirt. Marilyn was wearing yellow walking shorts and a white tank top.

Ken waved at me as I got out of the Blazer. "Noah."

Marilyn folded her hands in her lap and said nothing.

I waved back. "Did I catch you at a bad time?"

Ken shook his head. "Just getting some air."

Marilyn looked at me, hopeful but skeptical.

"I thought I'd fill you in on something," I said, leaning against one of the pillars that bordered the steps. "And tell you what the police are telling me."

They exchanged anxious glances with one another and then looked back to me.

I told them about my encounter with Randall and my conversation with Charlotte Truman. I left out the part about Kate using again and softened Randall's blackmail into simply pleading with his wife to cover for him. I didn't see how either of those two facts would help them anyway, and I didn't see the point in upsetting them further. I finished by telling them what Liz's thoughts were.

Ken leaned back on his hands. "So basically they are going to wait out Costilla?"

I nodded reluctantly. "Most likely. They will do some more checking based on what I learned, but there's really nothing else to go on. And, I've got to admit, Costilla's a good fit. Motive. History."

Ken shook his head and let out a long sigh. Marilyn put a hand on his arm, glancing at him. He tried to smile, but only got halfway there.

Marilyn looked at me. "What is your honest opinion, Noah?"

I shrugged. "I think that what the police are saying makes sense. I haven't found a whole lot to contradict their idea."

Her jaw tightened, and she shook her head. "What is your opinion? Are they right?"

"I'm not sure what I think," I said. "On one hand, like I said, Costilla is the best suspect. There is no reason to believe that he didn't do it, particularly with what we know about what he knew."

"But you're not sure," Marilyn said.

I didn't want to get caught up in a discussion about what my thoughts were. Their daughter had been murdered, and I didn't want to give them false hope. The facts were the most important thing. Maybe not the easiest to live with, but the facts were where the answers would be found.

"I'm not sure," I said carefully. "But the only reason I say that is because I've tried to keep an open mind. Anybody and everybody's a suspect, you know? The police hypothesis is better than anything I've come up with."

Ken leaned forward, his forearms on his knees, a look of angst and exhaustion on his face. "Is there anything else to look at?"

"Do either of you know anything about a key that Kate had with her?"

They both looked at one another, then back at me, shaking their heads.

"Emily gave me a key that Kate left at her place," I told them. "She didn't know what it was for. I have someone working on that now. But it may be nothing." I paused. "I'm also going to try and locate this other woman that Randall may have been involved with. Honestly, though, I don't expect her to be involved. Randall's pretty much been cleared."

Ken nodded sadly, and Marilyn lowered her eyes. It was clear to me that their daughter's death would gnaw at them for years. Their body language and facial expressions indicated a unique pain known only to families of murder victims.

Marilyn sat up suddenly and stared at her husband. "Why did you do it?"

Ken looked startled. "What?"

She stood, and I could see that the rims of her eyes were red.

"You arranged this whole goddamn thing," she said, waving her arms wildly. "With the police and the government! I said I didn't like it. It was too dangerous for her!"

Ken's face fell a little. "She was going to go to jail, Marilyn."

"At least she would've been alive," Marilyn said, crying now. "At least I could've gone and seen her!" A loud, violent sob forced its way out of her mouth, and she ran into the house.

Ken ran a hand over his face, his eyes glassing over. He stood and looked at me. "Sorry."

"No, don't be," I said, feeling awkward. "It's hard. I'm sorry I haven't been able to give you any real answers."

He nodded, the tears in the corners of his eyes clearly visible now. "Let us know what you find." He turned and walked into the house.

I left the Criers' home with the same hollow feeling I'd been carrying around since seeing Kate's lifeless face in the trunk of that car. I despised that feeling. I refused to let that be the only way I remembered Kate.

Whoever had taken the old Kate away from me was going to pay.

 **56**

I drove to the hospital to see if Carter could improve my mood.

He looked better. There was color in his skin, and the tube had been removed from his chest, leaving a lone IV line trailing into the back of his right hand. There were a couple of bandages in different spots and he was maybe a tad thinner, but he looked like Carter again.

"Please tell me you brought me some real food," he said, sitting up. "I can't eat this crap anymore."

"Sorry. Want me to get you something?"

"Hell, yes. The next time I see a tray come in here with covered things on it, I'm gonna jump out the window. Seriously." He looked at me. "You alright? You look like shit. And I don't mean from Costilla's beating."

I shook my head and sat on the edge of the bed. I told him about going to see the Criers and Marilyn's explosion at the end.

"The problem is," Carter said, "I have a hell of a time feeling sorry for them."

I looked at him. "Hey. Their daughter's dead. Easy."

He shrugged. "I'm sorry. It's hard for me to look at them as anybody other than the people that made you miserable."

"Your loyalty has its faults."

"No, it doesn't. I feel badly that their daughter is dead, but it doesn't make me like them any more than I ever did."

I didn't feel like having the conversation with Carter. He was grumpy and tired of being in the hospital, and regardless of his feelings for the Criers, I didn't want to hash it out there.

"How do you know Charlie?" I asked, moving us away from the subject.

"Charlie? Just a guy I run into now and then," he said.

"He's creepy."

"Yeah, a little, but he's alright."

"Think he'll be able to get me anything on that key?"

"If he can't, no one can."

I hoped that he could. I didn't know if it would lead to anything, but at the very least, it would be a closed loop in the mystery.

"You know yet when they are going to release you?" I asked.

He rolled his eyes and made a face at the door. "I wanted to leave today. I feel fine. But they want me here for one more night."

"Your charming personality, no doubt."

"Man, I have tried to piss off every person that walks in here, hoping they'll kick me out," he said, clenching his fists. "They keep telling me how they can't believe I've recovered this fast. And I'm like, I know, sign the goddamn release papers."

"That famous Carter charm must be working. They love you too much to let you go."

"Bite me," he said, shooting me a dirty look. "I want out." He took a deep breath and dropped back on the pillow. "What's the story with you and the Ice Queen?"

"I'm not sure you're in the mood to hear about it," I said.

He waved his hand around the room. "If I'm gonna have a heart attack, this is as good of a place as any."

I laughed and started to tell him, but my cell phone rang in my pocket. I pulled it out. "Hello?"

"Who's this?" the voice asked.

"Noah Braddock. Who're you?"

"Just checking," he said. "It's Charlie. I'm calling about your key."

"Right. What can you tell me?"

"That it's ready to be picked up, dude," he said, that hissing-laughing sound making its way out of his throat and through the phone line.

"Great. Did you find out what it belongs to?"

"Um, sir, your key is ready," he said again. "The cost is one fifty and I'll be at my desk the rest of the day. I can show you what you need to know."

I started to ask him again if he knew anything, but the line went dead. I closed up the phone and looked at Carter. "Your buddy, Charlie."

"What'd he say?"

"That my key's ready. Wouldn't tell me if he found anything."

Carter chuckled. "He's a little paranoid, Noah. A few irons in the wrong fire, you know? Is he charging you?"

I stood. "For the third time. Said it was going to cost me one fifty to pick up my key."

"If he's taking your money, then he knows where to stick that key."

I walked to the door. "He goddamn better, because if he doesn't, he's not gonna like where I'm gonna stick it."

 **57**

Charlie was in exactly the same pose I'd found him in before. He was in the middle of lighting a cigarette when he saw me coming.

He lifted his chin and blew out a huge puff of smoke. "You made it."

"You told me it was ready."

He sucked on the cigarette and brought his feet down off the ledge of his cart. "Yeah, sorry about that. Phones are dangerous, though, man. Never know who's listening."

"Right."

"Fucking government controls everything," he said, rummaging around in the drawer of the cart. "You think they don't know exactly what we're doing every minute of the day?" He tossed his ponytail over his shoulder and grinned sideways at me. " 'Specially a guy like me."

"Sure."

He looked at me for a moment, then shrugged as if I didn't understand and he didn't care either way. He produced a small white envelope from the drawer. "Here it is."

"What exactly can you tell me, Charlie?" I said, trying to remain patient.

He held the envelope up in his hand, wiggling it as his smile widened, his cigarette dangling from the corner of his mouth.

"I'm gonna pay you based on what you tell me," I said. "You tell me where that key goes, one-fifty's yours. You tell me nothing, you get nothing."

He pulled the cigarette from his lips and looked hurt. "Dude, you're Carter's friend. I ain't gonna jack you around. Shit, I was pretty sure I knew where this little girl went when you showed it to me this morning." He handed over the envelope.

I opened it. It contained the key and a small slip of paper with the number seven scrawled on it. I looked at him.

"Amtrak station," Charlie said, kicking his toe on the ground. "You know the old depot?"

"Yeah."

"One of the lockers there," he said, breathing out the cigarette smoke. "I can't tell you exactly which locker, but it'll be one with a seven in the box number. Seventeen, twenty-seven, one-oh-seven, something like that. Look for an empty lock and that baby'll open it."

"How do you know it's a seven?" I asked.

"Has to do with the serial number on the key," he said,

then grinned again. "I could tell you how it all works, but then I'd have to kill you." When I didn't laugh, the grin disappeared. "Hey, man, if it doesn't open a locker there, come back and I'll give you your money back. Like I said, I ain't gonna jack around a friend of Carter's." He shrugged. "But it's gonna open one."

I pulled the money from my wallet and handed it to him. "I believe you. Thanks."

He shoved the money in his pocket and squeezed the cigarette between his fingers. "Anytime."

As I walked away, I couldn't imagine another time that I might need Charlie's help, but I guessed it wouldn't hurt to be in with a key guy.

 **58**

The old Santa Fe Depot was downtown, a couple of blocks east of the harbor on Kettner. A Mission-style building with wide arches, built in 1915, it represented the old part of San Diego that seemed to be disappearing with the tremendous growth. It had undergone several renovations and now hosted not only the Amtrak trains that ran the coast, but also the trolley that connected the Mission Valley area with downtown San Diego and the Mexican border.

The station was filled in the early summer evening, primarily with tourists looking to ride out to the stadium or down to Tijuana. The noise of the hustle and bustle echoed off of the hundred-foot ceilings and worn wooden benches.

It took me half an hour of looking before I hit pay dirt. It was the next to last locker bank that I had left to look at. I had looked at seven others in various places in the station, none of them matching the key in my hand.

When I shoved the key in locker fifty-seven, the lock clicked, the key turned, and I opened the small metal door.

A brown paper bag had been squashed into the small, square receptacle, the top of the bag folded and rolled over. I pulled the sack out and nearly dropped it on the floor, its weight surprising me. I gathered the package under my arm and walked over to a nearby bench.

The first thing I saw when I opened the bag was money. Still wrapped in bands. I didn't count it, but I guessed it to be near the half million Costilla had told me he was missing.

A manila envelope was folded in half, slid in next to the stacks of money. I pulled it out and opened it. A piece of yellow legal paper was folded into quarters.

I unfolded it. I saw Kate's name signed in the middle of the page, and I froze. My stomach dropped and the hair on my neck stood at attention. I stared at her name for probably five minutes before I read what was above it:

I'm putting this here because I'm in danger. This isn't my money but I'm taking it. The person that I've taken it from won't miss it, I can promise you that. But it's not him that I'm afraid of. It's my husband that I'm afraid of. He doesn't love me and I don't love him. We've done things to hurt each other, both of us. But I want the marriage to end and he doesn't. Appearances. So I'm putting this here so it will be safe even if I'm not. If I get out, then no one will ever see this. If I don't, hopefully someone will figure all of this out.

I've made a lot of mistakes in my life—too many, in fact. Ones that have embarrassed me, ones that have embarrassed my family, ones that have screwed up everyone's lives. I don't want to do that anymore.

I'm doing something now that I hope will let me start again. Something good and something bad. The something bad is taking this money. The something good is helping to catch the man who this money belongs to. I know this doesn't make sense, but if you are reading this, then something's probably happened to me and maybe this does make sense.

I am almost done with what I have to do and then I can escape and start new. Leave the past behind. There's nothing good in my past to go back to, so I want to go forward. Only forward. I hope I'm able to do that.

I read the letter three times, a cold knot settling in my gut. Kate had been afraid of Randall. She'd put it on paper, just in case. She'd taken Costilla's money so she could get the hell away from him and try to rebuild her life.

But the thing that hit me the hardest was that she wanted to leave all of her past behind.

A past that included me.

It could have been Emily telling me that Kate mentioned me on her wedding day. Or perhaps it was

Ken's comment about Kate possibly looking for me. Or maybe it was me getting caught up in years of missing Kate and hoping she'd felt the same.

The letter crushed that hope with the force of a hammer to the chin, and it hurt badly.

A person sliding in beside me startled me. So did the gun in my ribs.

Ramon smiled, sitting at my side. "You've found Mr. Costilla's lost package. He will be very grateful."

Beyond Ramon, I saw the thick-headed man that had driven me to my meeting with Costilla in Tijuana. The outline of a gun under his shirt was well defined.

"You've been following me?" I asked, feeling ridiculously novice.

"Yes," Ramon said. "From a distance, of course. But, you see, Mr. Costilla, he figured you were the guy to help us. Like he told you."

I shifted on the bench and felt the gun press harder into my ribs.

Ramon nodded at the letter. "May I?"

I handed it to him. He read it quickly, then handed it back. "I guess I will only need the bag, unless there is anything else in there you need."

I shook my head. I didn't want to give up the money, but I knew the letter was more important. I wasn't going to lose another battle with Ramon and his friend.

I felt the gun pull away from my body.

Ramon reached for the bag and slid his gun down to the bench between our bodies so it was hidden. "Mr.

Costilla is grateful. He hopes that there are no hard feelings."

I looked at Ramon. "He didn't kill her, did he?"

Ramon shook his head sadly. "No, he did not, Mr. Braddock. He told you that. I can see why you wouldn't believe him. But he didn't." He nodded at me. "Good-bye." He tucked the bag under his arm, and he and the other guy disappeared out the door.

I sat there, my mind reeling. I heard a ringing in the distance as I stared at Kate's letter in my hands. I looked at the words, not reading them, but wondering how things had gotten so bad for her.

The ringing intensified, and I looked up from the letter, irritated that some idiot didn't realize his cell phone was ringing.

Then I realized I was the idiot.

I stuck the letter in my pocket and pulled out the phone. "Yeah?"

"We've gotta talk," Randall Tower said.

I stood up, gripping the phone tighter. "Fucking right we do."

"I need to talk to you," he said, and I realized he was drunk.

"Where are you?" I asked, heading for the door. "Because I'm coming."

"Meet me at the gliderport," he said, his words running together. "We can fly away together."

I hung up the phone and sprinted to my car.

 **59**

As I weaved in and out of the evening traffic on I-5, I called Liz on my cell.

"Guess what I found?" I said, when she picked up.

"What?"

I told her about the money and the note.

"Do you have it with you?" she asked.

"The note, yeah. The money, no."

"Where's the money? In the locker?"

"No, Ramon has it."

"Who the hell is Ramon?"

"Costilla's sidekick."

"Shit."

I passed a slow-moving van on the right as I flew past Old Town and Presidio Park. "I know. Nothing I could do, though. But you need to see the note."

"Yes, I do," she said. "There's something else you should know though."

"What?"

"Charlotte Truman's dead."

My chest tightened. "What? How?"

"Not sure. After you talked to her, I called a friend in LAPD and asked him to notify me if her name popped up in anything unusual. He just called. They found her in her hotel room." She paused. "A witness got a license plate leaving the hotel in a hurry."

"They run it?"

"Yeah, it was rented out of Lindbergh Field. By Randall Tower."

It was like I saw the punch coming but didn't bother ducking. "What a fucking surprise that is."

"Agreed. Where are you right now?"

"On the five, the La Jolla Parkway exit," I said, trying to block Charlotte's face from my mind.

"You going to see Carter?"

"No, I'm going to talk to Randall."

The line buzzed for a moment, and I knew she wasn't happy. "This isn't for you to handle."

"The fuck it isn't," I said. "I just got off the phone with the asshole."

"What? Why?"

"I don't know. He called me, said we had to meet. And I agreed."

"You need to wait for me. Or Wellton," she said. "He was on his way to Westwood to meet with the LA guys about Truman. I can call him on his cell."

"Randall called me, Liz," I said, gripping the steering wheel tighter. "I'm going to see him. And I'm not waiting. Come if you want, I don't care. But I'm not waiting."

"Where are you meeting?" she asked, the aggravation clear in her voice.

"He says he's up at the gliderport."

"Noah, don't do anything until one of us gets there. You got it."

"Bye," I said and clicked off the phone.

It rang again five seconds later. I figured it was Liz again, but the caller ID on the phone showed a number I didn't recognize. I punched the button. "Hello?"

"Dude," Carter said. "I'm starving. Where's my dinner?"

"Carter, I'm busy right now," I said, swinging the Blazer over into the far right lane. "I can't."

"What's going on?"

I told him what I'd found, what Liz found, and where I was headed.

"Wait for Liz," he said. "If you tear him up, there's gonna be nothing she can do."

"The letter's good enough," I said.

"No, it's not," he said. "It doesn't mean shit. Doesn't mean he killed her."

"She was afraid of him, Carter," I yelled into the phone. "She was hiding the money. Charlotte Truman is dead. Ramon told me again that they didn't kill Kate. I believe him."

"You believe Costilla's thug? Come on. You're not thinking, Noah."

I fired the phone at the passenger door. I took the La Jolla Village Drive exit and headed toward the Torrey Pines gliderport to find Randall Tower.

 **60**

The gliderport lurked just south of the long fairways of the Torrey Pines Golf Course, a giant clearing amidst the thick trees and ultra-modern buildings of the biotech corridor along Torrey Pines Road. It was a magnificent takeoff spot for the crazies who were into hang gliding, a flat clifftop that abruptly disappeared and sent them shooting out over Black's Beach, three hundred feet above the Pacific.

I turned down the paved road that ended in a cul-de-sac. Access to the dirt road and parking area was chained off, a sign proclaiming the port closed after eight at night. A blue Ford Taurus was parked next to the sign.

I parked the Blazer behind the Taurus and got out. I blinked several times, letting my eyes adjust to the darkness. I shivered into the cool wind that whipped up and off the cliff face, listening to the ocean roar in the distance.

I walked around the empty lot and down the narrow dirt road. I squinted into the night and barely made out a faint light up ahead where I knew the steep path down to Black's began. As I got closer, I heard whistling.

Randall was seated on the dirt landing at the top of the stairs, beneath the signs proclaiming the danger of the cliffs and the unstable path, his back to the ocean. A dim, single bulb light barely illuminated the signs, a whistling Randall, about eight empty beer bottles, and one ominous-looking syringe. His light blue oxford was untucked, the left sleeve rolled up above the elbow, and his khakis were wrinkled and dirty at the knees. He didn't seem to notice that just three feet to his left, the earth disappeared.

He was holding a bottle of Grey Goose in his hand, and he lifted it toward me as a greeting. "Hey, Mister Super Private Detective is here. Woohoo."

"Yeah, I'm here," I said, my jaw aching from the clench I'd placed it in since talking to him on the phone.

He made an exaggerated act of looking at his watch. "Well, it's about time." He wiggled the vodka bottle in the air. "Can I offer you a drink?"

I kicked the bottle out of his hand, and it went flying down the steep path, shattering somewhere down below. I grabbed him by the shirt and yanked him off the ground and to his feet.

"I don't want a drink, asshole," I said, jerking him closer so he could see my face. "And I don't want to share a needle, either. I want to know what you did to Kate."

His head lolled to one side, no fear on his face, just drunken, strung-out comfort in his glazed-over eyes. "Come on, man. Noah. Buddy." He smiled, his eyes half open. "Let's have one last beer together."

I spun him away from the stairs and threw him to the ground, his body hitting the dirt in front of the stairs like a bag of rocks.

He looked up at me, surprised, then pointed a finger at me. "You are so strong, man."

The anger erupted inside my chest, and I jumped on him, driving my fist straight down on his nose. It collapsed like a stepped-on snail, and he screamed, his voice echoing out over the water into the dark.

"Listen to me," I said, lowering my face next to his, my anger giving my voice an edge I didn't know it had. "I know you killed Charlotte Truman, and you're gonna tell me what you did to Kate. Or you are going over the side of this cliff and then I'm gonna come down and break everything that's not already broken."

"Charlotte," he slurred. "I didn't want to."

"I wanna know about Kate."

"You don't understand," he mumbled.

The blood from his nose looked purple in the dark. His eyes crossed as he tried to get a look at the damage in the middle of his face. He touched it with his hand, winced, and then clumsily tried to shove me off of him. I moved to the side, but kept a hand in the middle of his chest.

"Make me understand, Randall."

He knocked my hand away and rolled over awkwardly, and I stood up with him.

He turned around to face me, staggering a bit to his left. The blood leaked down his face onto his shirt. He tried to wipe his mouth with the back of his hand, but managed only to smear it onto his cheek.

"She made me do it," he said, sounding as if his mouth was full of gravel.

The anger surged again in my chest. "What?"

He looked at the blood on the back of his hand, then at me. "She made me do it, you dumbass."

I grabbed him again, spun him around, and pushed him back toward the top of the stairs and the edge of the cliff. He tried to push me away, but I didn't let go. He twisted around, trying to look behind him as I marched him toward the edge.

"Don't!" he said, his eyes moving wildly. "It's not my fault!"

I stopped about a foot short from where the edge gave way to a long, nasty tumble, the ocean groaning at the bottom. "All of this is your fault. All of it. You let Kate go down for your mistake." I jerked him toward me so we were chest to chest, my fists full of his shirt, pushed up under his chin. "And now you're telling me Kate made you do all of it? It was her fault?"

He blinked several times, and the fear that had shaped his face was gone. He looked at me for a moment, his hands dropping to his sides, giving up.

"You still don't get it," he said, almost laughing.

Anger streaked through my body, and I shook him hard, our foreheads banging together. "You're right! I don't!" I jerked on the oxford again and the buttons that ran down the middle popped loose and I stumbled a couple of steps back, a piece of the cotton fabric clutched in my right hand.

We stood there for a moment, both of us breathing heavily, the wind whistling around us. I looked at him, blood running from his nose onto his now exposed chest.

There was something so familiar about him.

Then I looked at the piece of shirt in my hand.

And that's when I finally figured it out.

"Don't move," a voice whispered in my ear, the cold barrel of a gun pressing into the back of my neck. "Don't turn around until I tell you to."

The voice should have startled me, but it didn't. I knew, staring at Randall, what I had been missing all along. I had been lulled into looking in the other direction, not looking right where I should have been all along. As I stood there, the voice whispering in my ear, my gun pulled from my waistband, I couldn't believe that I had missed it.

And now, as the ocean roared down below us, I figured I was probably going to miss the rest of my life.

 *61*

Emily Crier said, "Turn around slowly, Noah."

I did as she said.

"You two having fun?" she asked, pointing my gun at me. She tucked her gun into the waistband at the front of her jeans. "Looks like it."

I could only stare at her. Blond hair piled on top of her head. Black sweater and black jeans. Black sandals and black gloves. The blond hair was the only thing that made her stand out against the night.

Randall came up next to me, steadying himself against my shoulder. "I took care of Charlotte, Em. Like you wanted."

Emily didn't respond.

"And I didn't tell Noah anything," Randall said. "I swear."

She looked at him. "That's great to hear."

She moved the gun from me to him and shot him

twice in the chest, the shots echoing like cannon fire in the night.

Randall's eyes widened, his mouth open in a large, silent circle. He stumbled backward, clutching at his chest.

She fired again, hitting him where his hands were clawing at the first two wounds on his chest.

He looked at her, confused, took two more steps backward, his legs giving way, and tumbled over the ragged edge, disappearing from sight down into the unwelcoming water below.

I stared at the empty spot where Randall had just been.

I turned to Emily.

"You were the other woman," I said.

She laughed softly. "Brilliant."

"Randall's shirt," I said, holding up the blue fabric in my hand. "That was the same shirt you had on when I came to your place the other night. It wasn't your ex you were with. It was Randall."

"I hope my parents weren't paying you too much," she said. She motioned with the gun to move. "Nice and easy, okay? Move under the light where I can see you."

I dropped the piece of cloth and sidestepped slowly about fifteen feet to my right so that I was back under the dim light, next to the warning signs.

"Somebody's gonna find Randall," I said.

"I'll be gone," she said.

"They'll find you."

"No, they'll think you did it. Came here all pissed off and shot him." She smiled. "Your bullets, Noah."

"How long were you with Randall?" I asked, now wondering if there was any way I was going to survive.

"Too long."

"You love him?"

"Actually, yes, believe it or not. I loved him."

I processed what I knew. "But he wouldn't leave Kate."

She let out an irritated sigh. "That's right, Noah. He wouldn't leave her. Little Kate won again."

"Won again?"

She laughed. "Kate always won. Since we were kids. It got so damn old. Kate got everything she ever wanted."

"I don't think she wanted to die," I said.

She laughed again. "No, you're right about that."

"You killed her because Randall wouldn't leave her?"

She paused for a moment, as if she was considering what she was going to tell me. Then she gave a tiny shrug, like it didn't matter one way or the other.

"If you wanna put it that way, I guess I did," she said, rolling her eyes. "She decided to confront me before she went back home."

"Confront?"

"She found out about me and Randall," she said, smiling, her teeth biting into the darkness. "She listened to a message I'd left for him on his cell phone. A couple of weeks ago. She didn't go to Randall with it. She blamed me, and I guess it took her that long to get up the nerve to call me on it." She shook her head, clearly annoyed that her little sister was so weak. "So she called me up the night before she was supposed to go back to San Francisco, ranting and raving. I played dumb and offered to go down to the hotel to meet her that night. She was waiting for me in the parking lot, a little drunk and a little strung out. She started threatening me, telling me to stay away from Randall, and I had to make a decision. We were all alone." She nodded, as if she were affirming her decision. "It wasn't hard to do, and I felt better the second she stopped breathing."

The way she spoke, the way she recounted killing her sister, came off like she was reciting a grocery list. I knew she'd have no problem killing me.

"But more than anything, I just got tired of coming in second," she said, her eyes flashing. "Jesus, she even got out of the heroin thing."

"You put the heroin in the car?"

"No, I had Randall do it," she said, frowning. "That's one of the things I *made* him do, as he started to tell you. I wasn't touching that crap. But I knew she'd take the blame for him. Good little Kate."

We stood there on the clifftop, the water crashing below us, the dark sky getting darker by the second. A realization hit me.

"You introduced Kate to heroin," I said, staring at her.

Her frown shifted into a small smile. "That I did. She came to visit me my senior year at UCLA. A little weekend partying. Friend of a friend showed up with it. I never used it. But I wondered if she would." The smile on her face darkened. "She did, and she was in love."

I had family issues. Since I had never known my father, I guess it was just one issue—my mother. I wasn't sure that I loved her, but I didn't hate her, didn't have the sick anger that would make me look for ways to destroy her.

"You see," she said, shaking the gun at me, "Kate was always number one in our family. I was a distant second. Always. The only thing she ever did wrong was date you. I had to push her along, get a few more black marks on her record."

I glanced around, letting her talk. There was nowhere to go.

"I figured when she hit the heroin, that was it," she said. "Finally, she had done something that would make her look less than perfect. But, no. My parents . . . her parents . . . did everything possible to help her."

"And you didn't want to help her?" I asked her.

"I could've cared less," she said. "So when Randall and I started sleeping together, I knew I could finally have something of hers."

"But you couldn't."

"Oh, I would've," she said, smiling. "If you hadn't gotten into this. Let that Mexican guy take the rap. I could've gotten Randall to go my way. The heroin thing did a lot of damage to their marriage. It was over, and I think even Randall was finally ready to let it go." She paused. "But you just wouldn't let it go. My mother must've known you'd chew through steel for Kate."

"Why give me the key then?" I asked.

"I needed you to find that," she said. "When Randall started having guilt issues, I figured, fuck it. Let him go down. The key made Randall look like your man. I figured I'd kill him and make it look like a suicide." She shrugged. "I found the money and the note in Kate's car. Those were hers. I didn't fake those. I'm assuming you finally found them and that's why we're here. Only mistake I made was leaving Charlotte's name in the car. It was too much." She paused, her eyes tearing up. "And I thought it would work out, you know? Because you and I were starting something. Picking up where we left off eleven years ago."

All along, I knew that being with Emily never felt completely right. I'd thought it was because of the situation and because of the feelings I'd had for her sister. Instead, I realized that it was probably a gut reaction to the real Emily, the sick and screwed up Emily I was seeing now.

"But then you messed that up, too," she said, shaking her head. "That's when I knew this was where we'd end up."

"Here?" I said, waving my hand in the air.

"Figuratively," she said. "Randall called me in a drunken stupor, said he couldn't take it anymore. Was going to tell you about our affair. I knew you'd put it together."

"Did he know?" I asked. "That you were the one that killed Kate?"

She nodded, the gun still aimed in my direction. "I think he suspected me all along. He didn't flinch when I told him he had to take care of Charlotte. But he never confronted me. Too scared, probably." She laughed, but didn't mean it. "God, all this time and you are still worried about Kate. You never got it. You wanna know something about the love of your life?"

"Sure," I said, still looking for a way out.

"My parents never told her they wouldn't pay for Princeton," Emily said, her eyes flaring in the dark. "She made that up for you. She didn't want to hurt your feelings. She just wanted to go to college without a boyfriend."

I looked away, refusing to let her see that she had just hit me with an emotional machete.

"And she didn't ask about you on her wedding day," she said gleefully. "I came up with that one to soften you up." She shook her head, as if I was some kid who didn't get that Superman wasn't real. "You've spent all this time thinking about her, trying to figure out what happened to her, and you know what? She was done with you the last time she saw you."

I didn't know whether to believe her. Maybe she was trying to stick it to me like she had everyone else. But hearing those things, I knew that there was probably more truth than lie to her words, and I couldn't run and hide from them.

And now there was nowhere for me to go but into the ocean or into a bullet.

"So how does this end?" I asked, stalling again.

She lifted the gun, steadying it in her right hand. "I told you. You killed Randall. I'm going to kill you and then kick you over the edge." She smiled, the moonlight reflecting on her silver earrings. She pulled her gun from her jeans and aimed it at me with her left hand, cocked her right arm, and threw my gun over my head and over the cliff. She moved her gun to her right hand. "You two fought to the death."

"And you?" I asked. "What are you going to do?"

"Get the hell out of here," she said. "I've seen enough of this city and my family. I'll pretend to be distraught over all these deaths. It will make a nice excuse to look for a new beginning."

I wished briefly that I had told Liz about sleeping with Emily. At least there would've been something for her to look at when they found me. Carter would have to help her put it together.

"So, it's been nice, Noah," she said, leveling the gun at me. "It really has. I thought there might be a chance with us. But I should've known. You'd never settle for less than Kate."

I didn't raise my arms. I didn't duck. I just stood there, wondering what it would feel like to die.

 *62*

The shot came from behind Emily. It ricocheted off one of the metal signs next to me, the clang nearly deafening me.

Emily flinched, then turned and fired into the darkness.

I heard Carter yell, "Goddammit!" and then an unmistakable thud onto the dirt path.

I leapt at her. She came back toward me, and I swung my open hand at the gun as it came around. It went flying back behind to my left.

My momentum carried me into her, my shoulder hitting her in the chest, and we tumbled to the ground.

I reached for her, but she rolled to her right, creating a small cushion of space between us, and spun around toward the ledge. I pushed myself up and pivoted on my knees. I saw the gun near the edge of the cliff where Randall had fallen.

Emily scrambled to her feet, glanced at me, and charged for the gun.

I got up, took two steps, and dove for her. We collided in front of the gun, shiny and bright in the moonlight. I reached for it, and she bit down on my biceps. I screamed and reached for her with my other arm, but she slapped it away, her teeth sinking deeper into my flesh. I reached again with my free arm, found a handful of hair, and yanked back.

She yelped but managed to move forward toward the gun. I reached for her and grabbed at the waist of her jeans. We wrestled for a moment, and I twisted as I tried to pull her away from the gun. She looked back, her face tight with anger, and jammed her foot into my crotch. The air left my body, and I lost my grip on her.

I rolled onto my back and watched her get to her knees, reaching for the gun now near my shoes. She brought herself to her feet, squatted, and started to turn to me as she stood up, the gun barrel flashing in the moonlight as it came around.

The air wouldn't return to my body, a screaming pain burning its way from my groin to stomach. I knew I had one chance at not getting shot, and I knew either way the end result would be tragic.

As she turned, I watched her eyes, now completely unfamiliar to me. Fury raged in her face and body. I couldn't believe I'd been fooled.

I brought my knee back to my chest, then shot my leg at her as hard as I could, a deep, ugly grunt emerging from my mouth.

I caught her flush on the hip. Her body bent in half, then whipped back the opposite direction as she left the ground. The gun flew up in the air, and Emily flew over the cliff, her eyes still angry as she disappeared over the side.

 **63**

"We found them both on the rocks," Liz said.

She and I were back in the hospital the following morning. Carter was back in the bed, and we were sitting next to it. Carter had broken his arm, falling down while avoiding Emily's fire. He'd left the hospital after I'd called him, against doctors' wishes of course, but they couldn't stop him. If they had, I would've been dead.

I owed him, to say the least.

"Preliminary ballistics matches the bullet in Charlotte Truman to a gun we found in Randall's rental car," Liz continued.

Liz had arrived at the scene to find Carter sprawled in the dirt and me lying prone on the clifftop. She thought that I'd been shot. I didn't ask her how that made her feel because I figured the chances were fifty-fifty that I'd like her response.

"Her prints will probably be on the letter you found,"

Liz concluded. "That should close the deal." She looked at me. "We'll need to get a formal statement from you this afternoon. Probably take a couple of hours."

I glanced at her and nodded. "I'll come down."

She looked at Carter. "And if you'll get that how-itzer you call a handgun registered this week, I'll pre-tend it was registered when you used it last night." She gave him an I've-been-waiting-for-this-forever kind of smile. "And I promise not to tell the guys downtown that you fell down and broke your arm while shooting a gun."

"I was taking cover," he said, making a face. "It could happen to anyone."

"No," she said. "Just to you." She turned to me. "Can I see you outside for a second?"

I nodded, and we both stood. She looked back at Carter.

"I'm glad you are okay, Carter," she said. "And I'm glad you realized that your jackass of a friend was going to need some help."

"He is a jackass," Carter concurred, pulling at the sling on his newly broken arm.

Liz and I walked out into the hallway. She leaned back against the door to Carter's room, her eyes hard and sharp. She started to say something, then stopped.

"What?" I asked.

She pinched the bridge of her nose and shut her eyes. "Nothing. Just a lot to think about."

"I know," I said. "I can't believe she killed her sister. And Randall and Charlotte."

"That," she said, opening her eyes, "I can believe."

I looked at her, not understanding.

"What I can't believe is that you almost died last night." The corners of her eyes twitched. "You didn't listen to me. Again. You went to see Randall. You didn't wait for help. You nearly screwed up the whole thing." She paused. "Same old, same old."

I knew that my anger had gotten the better of me, but I wasn't sure how rehashing my mistakes was going to improve the situation.

I shook my head. "I don't know what you want me to say, Liz."

She stared at me for a moment, chewing carefully on her bottom lip. Her eyes were looking for something and apparently weren't finding it.

"I don't know either," she said finally.

She walked down the hall and disappeared around a corner.

I watched her go, unsure of what to do. I knew that I'd disappointed her. Maybe she thought that what had happened between us in the last couple of days was going to change me. I knew that it wouldn't, and yet I wasn't sure I was comfortable with that.

I walked back into the room.

"Is she really gonna tell them I fell?" Carter asked, frowning.

"What does it matter?" I asked, walking over to the window.

"My reputation will be shattered," he said, sounding

like a child who lost his favorite toy. "All that work to establish myself as a badass. Gone."

"You'll recover."

I felt his eyes on my back. "How are you?"

I stared out the window. The view was to the north, and I could see both Torrey Pines State Beach and the condos up on the hill where Emily had lived in the distance. "Fine."

"Really?"

"No. But I will be."

I knew that I would be, eventually. But death has a way of screwing you up. And not just the deaths of those around you, but the possibility of your own. I wasn't sure how long it would take me to find that sense of normalcy again.

"We should go do something," Carter said.

I turned back to him and looked at his cast and sling. "I don't know that you're in any kind of shape to be doing anything."

"They're gonna let me outta here tonight," he said. "But I mean doing something like getting out of town. Away from all this crap."

I liked that idea. "Okay. Where?"

He grinned. "I was thinking Cabo."

I nodded, again liking the idea. "Good choice."

"No Ice Queen," he said, raising an eyebrow. "Just me and you."

"No problem," I told him, thinking about what had happened out in the hallway with Liz. "Just me and you. And the trip's on me."

"As it should be," he said, the grin returning. "A little food, a lot of alcohol, and a lot of surfing."

"Your arm gonna be up for getting in the water?"

He made a face at the cast. "It'll be fine." He looked back at me. "Yeah. Cabo. Food, booze, and we'll surf until we're dead in the water."

I hadn't been to Cabo San Lucas in a couple of years. There was a strong right break known as Zippers just up the road from the resorts, on the Sea of Cortez side of the point, that produced solid waves and took a lot out of you on a good afternoon. I pictured the azure colors of the water, paddling out to the lineup, and leaving a lot of things out on those waves.

I was already looking forward to it.

Acknowledgments

This book may have my name on the cover, but it belongs to many others, and many thanks are owed. Mario Acevedo, Jim Cole, Heidi Kuhn, Margie Lawson, Tom Lawson, Sandy Meckstroth, Jeanne Stein, and Bob Stricker all read the book in its infancy and took the time to offer numerous suggestions that made it infinitely better. Victoria Sanders took me on as a client and made all of this happen—I will forever be grateful. The hardworking folks at Dutton—particularly Brian Tart, who was willing to take a chance on an unknown, and Martha Bushko, who in her wit and wisdom found the book I didn't know I'd written—have made the entire process more enjoyable and more enlightening than I ever could've hoped for. And to my wife, Stephanie, who endured countless hours of whining, moaning, and mood swings and still managed to provide plenty of encouragement, support, and kicks in the ass when they were required—you are simply the best person I know.

Read on for a preview of
Jeff Shelby's next
Noah Braddock mystery

WICKED BREAK

Coming from Dutton in July 2006

The man on the shore was waiting for me.

I'd been in the water for an hour, catching a nice southern break that was producing tight swells of about three to four feet just north of the jetty in Mission Beach. He'd been there for about half that time, watching from a distance, and when I dug the nose of my six foot Ron Jon into the face of an anxiety-free wave and went ass-over-kettle into the water, the distraction of being watched ended my session.

I trudged in, shaking the ocean out of my hair as I approached the shoreline. The beach was deserted on a cloudy Monday at mid-morning. When the man waved at me, I knew he wasn't trying to get anyone's attention but mine.

"Are you Noah?" he asked. "Noah Braddock?"

I ran a hand over my face, sliding away the excess water and not bothering to disguise a frown. I jammed the butt of the board into the sand and let it stand erect. "Yeah. Who are you?"

"I'm Peter Pluto," he said. "I need your help. I need you to find my brother." He gestured behind him. "The guy at your place said you were out here. Your roommate, I assumed."

Carter was not my roommate, but inhabited my place nearly as much as I did.

I studied Peter Pluto. He wore blue jeans and a brown sweatshirt with old running shoes. His thinning, dark hair was trimmed short and the lines in his face told me he hadn't slept much recently.

I bent down and undid the velcro leash around my right ankle. "That right?"

"You are an investigator, aren't you?" he asked, squatting down a little, trying to get even with my face.

I stood back up. "Yeah, I am. But I'm not doing a whole lot of work right now."

"I'll make it worth your while," Peter Pluto said. "Cash up front."

"It's not about the money, Mr. Pluto," I said. "I'm just not looking for work at the moment. Other things going on, you know?"

"Peter. Call me Peter." He blinked a couple of times and, for a moment, I thought he might cry. But he shifted his eyes and sighed. "I guess Mike Berkley was wrong."

I looked at him, surprised. "You know Berk?"

Pluto nodded. "Yeah. He handled my mother's estate when she died. That's how I got your name. Said you'd be able to help me."

Mike Berkley was an attorney who had thrown me some work when I first started out as an investigator. I was having a hard time paying the bills and he'd come through with some simple stuff that had kept me out of complete poverty. Berk had become a friend and I didn't think that he would've offered my name without reason.

"Tell me about your brother," I said, pulling my rashguard up over my head.

Pluto looked at me cautiously for a moment, perhaps wondering if I was serious. He relaxed when he saw that I was.

"His name is Linc and he's nineteen," Pluto said. "He's been gone for at least a couple of days."

"Have you gone to the police?"

He hesitated, something crossing in his eyes that I couldn't read.

"I don't think the police will do anything," he said. "He's legal and he's run away before."

"Run away?"

Pluto nodded. "About four years ago. Before our mom passed away. She had cancer and it was tough on him."

"Where were you?"

He shifted uncomfortably, kicking his right shoe into the sand. "Basically, I'd left him there. It was tough on me, too. I was going to school up at UCLA. I didn't make it home very often, I guess."

I nodded. "So where is he living now?"

"Up in the college area," he said, referring to the neighborhoods around San Diego State. "When Mom died two years ago, he was emancipated and has lived on his own since."

"How come not with you? Or your father?"

A small wave of anger spread across his face. "We didn't really have a dad."

I knew the feeling. I didn't push it.

"As for why Linc didn't live with me—well, he hates me." Peter Pluto gave a half-smile, sadness and shame creeping into his eyes. "Blames me for not sticking around and leaving him with her. When she died, I tried to get him to come live with me. But he wouldn't do it. There was a small trust from our grandparents. He's managed to make it last for a while. Won't take my help."

"But now you want to help."

He nodded. "I check up on him once a week. Knock on his door, he tells me to fuck off, at least I know he's alright. I went there Friday and no one answered. Tried Saturday and yesterday. Nothing."

"How do you know he didn't just take off for a few days?" I asked. "A little vacation or something."

Pluto shook his head sternly. "That's not him. He's going to State, majoring in political science. Wants to be an attorney, I guess. Plus, it's almost midterm time."

"Midterms usually . . . mean bigger parties at State," I said, scoffing at the notion that anyone took exams seriously up on Montezuma Mesa.

Pluto shook his head.

"Maybe he needed to blow off a little steam," I said. "Get away for a day or two."

"He doesn't do that kind of thing. He's serious about school."

I thought Peter was kidding himself. San Diego State is the bastard child of San Diego universities. It lacks the private prestige and pricey tuition of USD and doesn't come close to the scientific reputation of UCSD. The students who ended up there did so because they were denied admission to the other two schools or simply because they didn't want their studies to get in the way of partying.

As an undistinguished alum, I knew that from experience.

"Your best bet is still to report it to the police," I said. "Even if he's run away before, you can file a missing persons report. I can give you the name of someone who will listen to you and take you seriously."

Whatever had crossed his eyes before when I'd mentioned the police was back.

"I can't go to the police," he said.

"Why not?"

He took a deep breath and shoved his hands into the pockets of his jeans. "I went into his apartment, okay? I talked the super into letting me in yesterday because I was worried." He stopped, his face tightening. "And I found something."

I didn't say anything.

"There were guns in his dresser," Peter Pluto finally

said. "A ton of them. I don't know anything about guns, but there were some that looked like handguns and some that looked like things I've seen in movies. Automatics, maybe, like machine guns. I freaked out and left."

I flicked a bead of water off my arm. Peter wasn't doing much to convince me to find his brother. "So he's not totally serious about school, I guess."

He yanked his hands out of his pockets, his face coloring. "He must have gotten hooked up with a bad crowd. Look, he's had a tough time with everything that's happened." The color receded from his face and a look of utter frustration and concern replaced it. "If he needs help, I want to help him. But I don't want him to go to jail." He stared at me with desperate eyes. "Mike said you could help. Can you?"

I gazed at Peter Pluto for a moment. The last time I'd gotten involved in a family affair, I'd been shot at, Carter nearly died, and I pushed a woman to her death. I didn't want to wade into that kind of mess again.

But I'd lied about not needing work. Truth was, I hadn't seen any good money in awhile. A new Jeep payment and a surf trip to Cabo had eaten quickly through my small savings account. I was going to need to do something soon.

Maybe this wouldn't be so personal, though. Do the work, find the kid, get paid. I didn't know Peter or his brother. I figured my past would have a tough time getting in the middle of this one.

And there was something about standing on a quiet

beach under thick gray clouds with a man who clearly cared about his brother that made me vulnerable.

"Give me the address," I said to Peter Pluto.

I asked Peter a few more questions about the guns he'd seen because I wanted a better idea of what I might be getting myself into. But he clearly knew nothing about guns and the tension on his face told me that finding them had shocked the hell out of him. I knew I'd have to go look for myself. He gave me a wallet-size photo of Linc and I told him I'd be in touch after I checked out the apartment.

I went back to my place, dropping my board on the patio that faced the beach. Carter had apparently anticipated my irritation with him and vacated the premises. Not as dumb as he looked.

I showered and changed into a pair of corduroy board shorts and a T-shirt. I grabbed an apple and a soda out of the fridge and headed out to see where Linc Pluto lived.

I pointed my Jeep east, going past the Bahia and the bay, getting onto Interstate 8 behind the old Sports Arena. The freeway cut through Mission Valley, bisecting the giant canyon that now housed a golf course, several shopping centers, and QualComm Stadium. I merged south on the 805, the canyon walls now closer to the freeway, and took the second exit, College Avenue.

The area around San Diego State was trying to reinvent itself, just like other older parts of the city. The university wanted to sell itself as a destination school rather than a state school and they were hoping to create a college town feel. Abandoned strip malls had been rebuilt with fast food joints and cafes. But the new neon of the signs in the windows hadn't deterred those who had been used to the old ways of the neighborhood. You were safe during the day, but you didn't venture out at night unless you were with your frat pals.

I found Linc's address just past the old Aztec Drive-In. It was an ugly L-shaped, two-story building, with an old asphalt lot in front. The stucco exterior was painted drab brown and the doors were a shade darker. Could've been an old motel.

I parked in the lot and found Linc's door on the ground level. A small window sat just to the right of the door.

I knocked, but got no answer.

I tried the door, but it didn't open.

I looked in the window, but saw no one.

Nowhere fast.

I walked down to the next door. Bob Marley crooned softly behind it.

I knocked.

Footsteps came closer and the door swung open.

A girl about twenty or so stood in front of me. A tight olive tank top hugged the curves of her chest, cut off cargo shorts exposed long tan legs. Her hair was a mess of dirty brown dreadlocks piled on top of her head. The thin silver hoops in her earlobes matched the ones in her eyebrow and nostril. She was attractive in an I'm-in-college-and-rebelling kind of way.

Her emerald eyes flashed and she looked annoyed. "What?"

"I'm looking for your neighbor."

"Did you try his place?"

I smiled. "Yeah. He's not there. Any idea where I could find him?"

She folded her arms across her chest. "Who are you?"

"Noah Braddock. I'm an investigator. Who are you?"

"Dana Madison." She looked at me with new interest. "An investigator. No shit?"

"None whatsoever."

"And you're looking for Linc?"

"I am."

"Well, I don't know where he is," she said. "But Rachel might."

"Rachel?"

"My roommate." She looked me up and down with a confidence she couldn't possibly have been old enough to possess. A slow smile emerged on her face and she stepped to the side. "Right this way, stud."

I felt dirty, but in a good way, and stepped past her into the apartment.

Dana went and turned down the stereo in the corner. The interior was sparsely furnished and the white paint on the walls was cracking. The aroma of freshly smoked marijuana filled the room. A small television sat on a banged up hutch. A worn wooden coffee table stood in the middle of the room just across from a tattered brown sofa. A Donald Duck bong grinned at me from the tabletop.

First Pluto, now Donald.

Disney appeared to be overtaking my life.

"You see where the spout is on him?" Dana said, coming over to the sofa and noticing I was looking at Donald.

"Uh, yeah."

"Makes it look like you're giving him a hummer when you spark up."

"Cool."

"I know," she said, missing my sarcasm.

"So. Rachel?"

Dana nodded, still looking at me. "You have to be in such a hurry?"

"Busy, busy."

A smile curled onto her lips. "I'd like to see you get busy." She turned toward the hallway that extended off the room and yelled, "Rachel. Somebody here for you."

A scuffling sound came from down the hallway, followed by footsteps. Rachel emerged.

If Dana was attractive, Rachel was a flat-out knockout. A fiery mane of red hair cascaded around her tan, oval face. She wore jean shorts frayed at the ends and a tight black top, exposing a drum-tight abdomen and a tiny diamond in her navel. Her arms and legs were as tan as her face, toned like her stomach. The only imperfection I could see was that her large brown eyes were ringed with bright red blood vessels.

She looked at me, confused. "Hi."

"Hi."

"This is Noah," Dana said. "He's a private investigator."

Rachel gave me a blank stare. "Oh."

"I'm looking for Linc," I said. "Next door."

"Oh."

"You know him?"

"Yeah she does," Dana said, then giggled.

Rachel looked at her. "Yeah I do." Then she giggled. Stoners can be frustrating.

I took a deep breath. "How do you know him?"

Rachel folded her arms across her chest. "From school."

"And you guys are friends?"

"Yeah they are," Dana said and snickered again.

"Shut up," Rachel said to her, then laughed again as well. She composed herself quickly. "We're friends."

"Friends?"

Rachel blinked several times. "He tutored me."

Dana laughed out loud and rolled onto her side on the sofa.

"Tutored?" I asked.

Rachel looked down at her feet. "Sorta."

I took another deep breath and tried to relax. "Look, Linc is missing. I'm trying to find him. He's not in trouble. And I don't care about the pot or anything else you two probably have stashed in here. Just be straight with me."

It was quiet for a moment while they tried to process what I said.

"Just tell him," Dana finally said.

"Shut up," Rachel said, looking at her.

"He's not from the school," Dana said, frowning at her friend. Then she looked at me. "Right? You aren't some kinda school cop?"

"I'm not."

She looked back at Rachel. "See?"

Rachel frowned at her friend, but didn't say anything.

Dana turned back to me. "Linc wrote papers for her."

"Dana! Shut up!" Rachel said, her cheeks flushing slightly.

"And she fucked him in return," Dana said, smiling.

"You bitch," Rachel said, shaking her head.

College had apparently changed since I'd been enrolled.

"It wasn't just like that," Rachel said to me.

"Okay," I said. "I'm not looking for an explanation. I just want to find him."

Rachel's cheeks continued to flush. "I mean, I can't write very good. He offered to help. And it just kinda . . . happened."

"Just once?"

Dana laughed.

"Well, no," Rachel said. "A couple times. But not recently. The last time was like two months ago. I swear."

"Alright. When did you see him last?"

She thought about it, lines forming above her perfect eyebrows. "Two days ago."

"Any idea where he might be?"

She shook her head slowly. "No. Do you think he's in trouble?"

"No idea," I said, wishing I hadn't knocked on their door. I pulled a card from my pocket and held it out. "If you hear from him or think of anything, call me."

Dana lurched off the sofa. "Can I get one of those?"

I reluctantly withdrew another one and handed it to her.

She smiled at it, then winked at me. "Thanks, stud."

I left before my head exploded.